BAD GIRL TRAINING

(THE UNDERCOVER FILES, #2)

JESSICA SORENSEN

Bad Girl Training

Jessica Sorensen

All rights reserved.

Copyright © 2017 by Jessica Sorensen

For information: jessicasorensen.com

Cover design by MaeIDesign

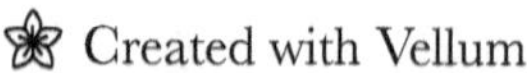 Created with Vellum

STUCK IN DREAMLAND

I'm having the best dream ...

I'm driving in the car with Benton and Jackson. Benton is in the back seat, and Jackson is driving. The radio is on, the windows are down, my shoes are kicked off, and my bare feet are propped up on the dashboard. The strange thing is that I know it's a dream. I don't know why or how I know this, other than maybe it feels too good to be true.

"I don't ever want to wake up from this," I admit as I stick my hand out the open window.

Benton scoots forward and brushes my hair away from my shoulder. "Then don't." He dips his head and places a soft kiss on my neck. The most wonderful shiver tickles across my skin, and I angle my head back. "You feel so good ..." he murmurs. "But your skin is so cold."

"That's not weird, though …" I sound dazed and far away, lost in dreamland.

Maybe that's exactly where I am. Lost. Perhaps I've been lost and dreaming since the night of Benton's party. Maybe none of what happened afterward was real. Part of me is relieved at the idea. That I didn't meet Axel, the drug lord. That I didn't hear him say he knew my mom. That I didn't vaguely recognize his colleague. That I didn't get tranquilized. But the other part of me is disappointed. Because if I did dream everything, then that means I never met the Bad Boy Rebels, which is quite possibly the most exciting thing that's ever happened to me. And as scary as the last twenty-four hours have been, I've secretly enjoyed the excitement. Have I been terrified? Absolutely. But I also liked the feeling, the adrenaline rush, the thrill of doing something out of the ordinary. What that says about me, I'm unsure. But I'm not about to overanalyze myself while I'm hanging out in one of the best dreams ever.

Benton places another kiss on my neck before chuckling and dropping back down in his seat. Then he smirks at Jackson.

Jackson rolls his eyes. "What? You think I'm impressed? I'll show you impressed." With a wicked glint in his eyes, he leans over the console and seals his lips to mine.

My heart flutters in my chest like a cracked-out hummingbird as he parts my lips with his tongue—

The car gives a harsh jerk, and his lips leave mine.

When I open my eyes, I'm alone, and the car is spinning out of control, heading for the river.

"Tell me, Zhara, have you ever tasted the poison of the devil? Because your mom sure did," Axel's voice flows through the car like a haunted memory.

"You don't know my mom," I whisper as I fumble to open the console so I can pop out the shoulder straps before the car crashes. But the big, red, for-emergencies-only button isn't inside. "No." I panic as the car starts to slide over the edge and toward the river. "This can't be happening."

"Yes, it can," Axel's voice echoes around me. "Look at you. You're so much like your mom. I bet you liked the taste of the devil's poison."

"No!" I scream, throwing my hands over my ears. "Just shut up—"

The car tumbles sideways and lands in the water. Metal bends. Glass shatters. A piercing pain stings my leg.

"No ..." My voice sounds so far away. "I don't want to taste it. I don't want to—"

"Zhara, open your eyes," a soft, welcoming voice slices through the water rolling over my body. "Come on; you need to wake up."

"I'm trying," I say on a whimper as water rises to my chin. "But I can't breathe ..."

"Yes, you can," the voice whispers. "Just take a deep breath and open your eyes."

I do what the voice says, inhaling and exhaling over and over again, and then I will my eyes to open. But my eyelids are too heavy, the water's too deathly cold, and my body is too exhausted.

"I'm dying," I whisper before the water carries me out of the car.

I'm not sure if I'm dreaming anymore ...

RETURNING TO THE LAND OF CONFUSION

I bolt upright and suck in a sharp breath, fighting to breathe.

Water. Water is everywhere.

I flail my arms around, trying to swim, when a hand touches my arm and confusion douses over me. Wait. If I'm in the water, then why is someone touching me? And why can I breathe?

I force my eyelids open, but my vision is blurry, making it nearly impossible to tell where I am. I blink several times and attempt to calm down.

"Good. Now take a deep breath," someone says from beside me.

I can't make out their face, but the deep voice has to belong to a guy. Maybe one of the Bad Boy Rebels? Or did Axel get ahold of me? Is that why I heard him in my dream?

I try to recall the last thing that happened before I was sucked into dreamland.

Standing on the side of the road. In the dark. Benton and Jackson beside me. That's where everything gets hazy.

"Where am I?" I croak out, continuing to blink. "And what time and day is it?"

"You're at Benton's. It's been a few hours since you passed out," the soft, deep voice says. "Don't worry; you're safe."

Gradually, my vision comes back into focus. I realize I'm sitting in a bed in an unfamiliar bedroom with dark blue walls. "Whose room is this?"

"It's Benton's."

My head snaps to the right, and I find Ridge sitting on a chair beside the bed, his eyes full of concern.

"Oh." I rub my forehead then wince from the pain. "Why does it feel like I've been run over by a truck?"

Keeping his gaze glued to me, he slants forward and rests his elbows on the edge of the bed. "Just how much do you remember?"

My shoulders feel heavy as I shrug. "I don't know … Being on the side of the road with Benton and Jackson. That's about where my memory cuts off."

"From what Benton told me, that's about when you passed out." He scoots the chair closer to the bed. "Do you remember why you passed out?"

My gaze falls to my leg, and I lift off the blanket covering me. I'm still wearing the cut-off shorts and the tank top Jackson tore, but the plaid jacket I had tied around my waist is MIA, along with the ring Axel gave me—thank God.

"I was tranquilized by a crazy drug lord, right?" I frown at the gnarly bruise on my leg. "That's gross." I can't even remember the last time I had a bruise, which seems a bit strange when I really think about it.

"The bruise is from the injection," he explains. "It should go away within a few days."

I start to relax when another thought occurs to me. "Wait. What time is it?" I cast a quick glance at the window, noting the stars and the moon are shining in the sky. "Crap, Loki's going to be so worried about me. I need to call him." I reach for my pocket to get my phone, but it isn't in there. "Crap, I must have dropped my phone somewhere."

Ridge gently places a hand on my knee. "Relax. Benton used your phone to text Loki and told him you were spending the night at Taylor's. And I'm sure he probably accidentally took your phone when he left."

"Oh." I exhale in relief. "I'm glad he did that. Loki

isn't used to me coming home late, and I'm sure he would've freaked out." I search for a clock to see what time it is. When I find one, my gratitude for Benton doubles. It's after one in the morning. Loki definitely would've been worried. "I just hope Taylor doesn't try to text me for a ride. I was supposed to call her a cab if she needed one. By now, though, I'm sure she's probably gotten one herself. She's going to be mad at me for letting her down."

"That doesn't really sound fair."

"Well, I told her I would pick her up or get her a cab, so …" I shrug. "It was sort of my responsibility."

He nods but doesn't seem convinced.

He runs his fingers through his messy brown hair, seeming stressed. His jeans and T-shirt are a bit wrinkled, and through his glasses, I spot bags under his eyes.

"You look tired," I note. "Is everything okay?"

He stares at me with his brows knit. "You just woke up from getting tranquilized and one of the first things you say is *I* look tired?"

I give a shrug, unsure whether he's complimenting me or if he just thinks I'm crazy. "I'm just worried maybe you stayed up too late while keeping an eye on me or whatever it is you're doing in here."

"I'm fine," he assures me, fidgeting with a tiny hole in his jeans. "I've actually been running on about three hours of sleep for the last three days or so, but that has nothing to do with you."

"Oh." I tuck a few stray strands of hair behind my ear. "What does it have to do with then?"

"The job, mostly. But I've also been dealing with some family drama." He frowns, but then he straightens and pats the bed. "How about you scoot over here so I can check you over before Benton texts *again*."

"Okay." I slide to the edge of the bed and lower my feet to the floor. "Where did Benton go anyway?"

He opens the top drawer of the nightstand and retrieves a thermometer and a pulse and oxygen meter. "He had to go do a work thing, but he's been texting about every five minutes to make sure you're okay." He takes my hand, his fingers slightly trembling as he positions the pulse and oxygen meter onto my finger.

Is he nervous? Why? Does it have anything to do with me mentioning Axel knowing my mom? From what I recall, I blabbed that detail to Jackson and Benton before I passed out.

Axel.

My mom.

Axel knows my mom.

The mantra fills my head, making my brain throb and my heart twinge. But I tell it to shut the heck up; that it can't be true.

"I need you to try to breathe as normally as you

can." Ridge pushes to his feet and slowly leans in toward me with the thermometer in his hand. "I'm going to put this in your ear and take your temperature. Try to hold as still as possible, okay?"

I nod and do as he asked, again noticing the unsteadiness in his movements, and again questioning if his nervousness has to do with Axel saying he knows my mom. Then another concern occurs to me. Are the guys going to kick me out over the possibility that my mom had a connection with a drug lord?

Stop thinking that! It's not true. Your mom wouldn't ever associate with a man like Axel.

But no matter how hard I try, I can't forget the memory of me driving in the car with my mom and a man I'm pretty sure works for Axel.

I swallow the lump wedged in my throat. "Ridge …? Did Jackson or Benton mention anything I said before I passed out?"

He positions the thermometer in my ear. "They said you passed along a message from Axel … And that you said something about him mentioning your mom."

"Oh." I don't know what else to say, so I keep my lips sealed and stare at my hands.

My heart hurts. My head hurts. Even my soul hurts a little bit.

"Zhara, you need to understand something about this world." Dipping his head, he catches my gaze. "A lot of crazy stuff happens. People you thought were your friends end up betraying you." He swallows hard, as if recollecting a painful memory. "Even your family can stab you in the back. And there are a lot of liars. And those liars will destroy weak people to get what they want, so you never know what's true and what's not."

"You think I'm weak?" I ask then shake my head. Of course he does, because I am. Always have been.

He firmly shakes his head. "Not at all, and that's why I'm telling you this—so you can learn what to watch out for." He uses his free hand to brush a few strands of my hair out of my eyes. "After what happened on your very first day, I'd be a complete idiot if I thought you were weak." He offers me a small smile. "You're a lot braver than most people and way braver than me."

I shake my head. "I don't think that could possibly be true."

"Don't doubt it. I kickass with anything that has a computer chip for a brain. But put me in a situation where I actually have to talk to a person, I lock up."

"You mean, you get stage fright?"

"Yeah, I guess you could look at it that way, but I'm not really on stage."

"Well, technically no, but you're acting, right? At least, that's how I felt when I was in the car with Axel. I didn't even feel like I was Zhara anymore." Honestly, I don't feel like her now, but that might be the drugs lingering in my system.

"Yeah, I've heard some of the guys say something similar." He removes the thermometer from my ear when it beeps. "I think looking at it that way makes it easier for them to do some of the shadier things the job requires."

"What sort of shady things?" I ask, partly curious and partly worried. What if they've killed people?

"Nothing as severe as what you're thinking," he says, his lips quirking.

"Hold on. How did you know what I was thinking?" I cover my mouth with my hand and let out an exaggerated gasp. "Wait. Was that really a mind reader doohickey you just put in my ear?"

He chuckles, glancing at the temperature on the thermometer. "Nah, I left that at home today." His brows dip. "Huh? So, it didn't go up."

"What didn't?"

"Your temperature … It's 97.5, which is slightly out of the normal body temperature range."

"Oh, I'm always like that," I tell him with a dismissive wave. "I have been for as long as I can remember."

He meets my gaze, a crease visible between his brows. "Have you ever talked to a doctor about it?"

"No, but I also haven't been to a doctor since I was, like, six."

"Really?"

"Yeah, I don't get sick very often. In fact, I think the last time I was actually sick was when I was six."

He scratches his forehead. "And did the doctor mention you having a low body temperature?"

"I can't remember. But I do remember my mom mentioning it a few times and telling me that, if anyone ever said anything about it, to tell them it was normal and that I was okay." I pause, noting how puzzled he looks. "Was she wrong? Am I not okay?"

"No, you're fine." His gaze descends to the pulse and oxygen meter. "Your pulse looks great, along with your oxygen level."

"That's good then, right?" Because it doesn't seem like he thinks it's good.

He forces a smile as he fixes his gaze on me. "Yeah, that's a good thing."

"Okay." I may not know him well, but I swear he's keeping something from me.

Before I can press for details—that is, if I could even figure out how to press someone I barely know—Wilder strolls into the room, wearing different clothes from the last time I saw him. He's now sporting a pair of dark jeans, a grey T-shirt, and clunky boots decorated with thick buckles. His blond and blue hair is a tousled mess on the top and, as always, his long eyelashes make him appear as if he's wearing eyeliner.

When his gaze falls on me, a smile lights up his face. "You finally woke up."

I plaster on a fake smile and nod, but the movement feels like a lie. The truth is, while I know I'm awake, I don't feel that way at all. In fact, I feel like I'm wandering around in a confused, sleepy dreamland where nothing makes sense because nothing is real.

DEVIL'S POISON

After Ridge is finished playing nurse—which, as it turns out, his mom is the real deal and that's how he has all the medical equipment—he instructs Wilder to get me something to eat.

Wilder has a few choice words to tell Ridge for trying to boss him around but eventually heads out of the room to, as he put it, "go whip me up a lovely feast."

Before he walks out of the room, though, he shoots Ridge a dirty look. "I'm only doing it for Zhara, not because you bossed me around." He smirks. "And now you owe me a favor."

"Sounds good," Ridge replies calmly, like a freakin' patience wizard guru or something.

After Wilder exits the room, I turn to Ridge. "I can

do the favor for you," I tell him. "He's getting the food for me."

Ridge's lips quirk as he puts his doctor tools back into the top nightstand drawer. "Thanks for the offer but trust me; you don't want to owe Wilder a favor."

"Why? How bad are they?"

"They're not necessarily bad, but they're not necessarily good either. Like, one time he made me pose for him for a still life, art project he was doing. He made me hold my computer while I was doing it, too, in the air, like a torch."

I giggle at the mental picture. "That doesn't sound too awful."

He takes a seat in the chair, sitting right across from me. "I had to stand still for over four hours. He wouldn't even let me have bathroom breaks. I seriously pissed my pants a little bit."

I try not to laugh, but the image of Ridge standing like the Statue of Liberty for four hours and trying not to pee his pants while Wilder painted him is sort of funny.

Ridge sighs, but a trace of a smile graces his lips. "Go ahead and laugh. Everyone else did."

I bite down on my lip. "I'm not trying not to laugh."

He gives me a *really* look. "Then, why are you biting your lip so hard?"

I shrug. "I'm hungry, and I have cherry lip gloss on,

so I thought, what the heck, maybe chewing on my lip will help my hunger."

Yep, and there's my awesome lying skills making a grand appearance. Jeez, after having to lie to a drug lord, you'd think I'd be able to lie like a pro by now, but nope.

He momentarily gapes at me then starts laughing. "You're kind of a little weirdo, aren't you?"

"You really think so?" I question. "Because I've always been told I'm rather ordinary and boring."

He shakes his head. "No way. I've only been talking to you for about twenty minutes and you already got me to laugh. I don't do that a lot."

"Well, that's just sad," I tell him. "I think I'll try to get you to do it more often."

He smiles, but confusion resides in his eyes. "You're different from what I was expecting." He dithers, chewing on his bottom lip. "Don't take this the wrong way, but considering who your friends are, I thought you were going to be stuck-up and kind of ditzy."

"Really? Not a know-it-all?"

He shakes his head. "Not at all. You never seemed like that."

"Well, that's what everyone else seems to think of me."

"Well, I've never thought about you." He smiles. He has a nice smile. Sweet and not at all dangerous looking like the rest of the smiles I've seen lately.

Granted, not all of those dangerous smiles were bad to look at either.

Beep. Beep. Beep.

"What's that?" I ask, sitting up straighter.

Ridge's eyes widen. Then he lets out a series of very colorful words as he springs to his feet and collects his computer. When he looks at the screen, he visibly relaxes.

"It's okay. It's just a false alarm." He sits back down and places the computer on his lap.

"What is it?" I want to look at the screen but worry it might make me come off as rude. But then he turns the computer toward me anyway.

"I'm tracking Benton, Xavier, and Jackson," he explains, pointing at three blue dots on a map of roads, rivers, and mountains. "This is their current location."

"Is that Honeyton?" I lean forward to get a better look.

He nods. "But if they were to leave Honeyton, the map would change to show wherever they were."

"That's cool." I examine the map. "So, right now, Benton, Xavier, and Jackson are down by the cemetery." That seems a bit strange. Do drug lords typically hang out at cemeteries?

Perhaps if they're burying dead bodies.

I shiver at the thought, which causes Ridge to glance up at me.

"Are you cold?" he asks worriedly. "Maybe you should lie back down and pull a blanket over you. I could have Jackson make you some soup. And hot chocolate."

"I'm fine," I promise. "I can eat whatever Jackson brings me."

"Are you sure? With what happened, I don't want you overdoing yourself."

Worry stirs in my chest. "Will there be side effects?"

He shakes his head and strands of his brown hair fall into his eyes. "There shouldn't be. In fact, normally when someone gets injected with devil's poison, they're fine within minutes of waking up." His brows furrow. "But with how long you were out, I want to keep a close eye on you. And your body temperature."

The hairs on the back of my neck stand on end. "Devil's poison?"

"It's the name of the tranquilizer Axel injected in you," he says then hurriedly adds, "Don't worry; the name sounds worse than it really is."

"Oh …" My heart pounds deafeningly inside my chest.

Ridge must notice my sudden uneasiness because he asks, "Zhara, what's wrong?"

"It's nothing." I fidget with the hem of my shorts. "It's just that, when Axel whispered into my ear, he said something about how my mom liked the taste of devil's poison."

"Oh." He grows quiet. Like really, really uncomfortably quiet.

I don't want to ask, but I feel like I have to. "Can people get addicted to it?"

"It's sort of becoming a growing problem and part of the reason we were put on this job. But honestly, the addiction usually isn't a choice."

"What do you mean?"

He wavers with uncertainty. "It means that the people who usually get addicted to it are being forced to take the drug, either through experiments or simply because people like Axel use it as a form of punishment."

"Oh." My heart thrashes in my chest as a single thought races through my mind.

Was my mom addicted to devil's poison?

"You don't need to worry. You won't get addicted from one dose," Ridge says, misinterpreting my silence.

"I wasn't really worried about that," I tell him. "I was just thinking, or more like wondering, if my mom was addicted to it and maybe that's why Axel said she liked the taste of it."

He hesitantly takes my hand. "Remember what I said about people in this world lying. Well, Axel is definitely one of those people who would lie to you, so I don't think you should stress yourself out about it."

"But, what if he was telling the truth?"

"If we find out he was, then we'll worry about it then. But there's no point in worrying about things if you aren't sure they're even true. It's a waste of time and energy."

"Okay, I'll try to stop," I tell him. But I'm unsure if I can. It's just not really in my nature. Although, sometimes I wish it was.

"Good." He gives my hand a squeeze, but then creases line his forehead. "God, your skin is so cold." He pauses, deliberating something. "I know you said it's normal for you to run this cold, but maybe we should run some tests."

I squirm at the idea of being prodded and poked. "What sort of tests?"

"Nothing too severe, I promise," he reassures me, moving the computer aside. "Just some bloodwork; that's all."

"And you'd do it?" I ask. "I wouldn't have to go to a hospital?"

He nods while studying me carefully. "I can draw the blood, then have my mom run the tests … Do you not like hospitals?"

"I don't know." My gaze lowers to my hands as my eyes sting with tears. I stare at the lines in my palms, willing the tears to go away, but instead, memories press at my mind.

When I was younger, my mom went through a phase where she decided she was going to learn how to palm read. She practiced on Alexis, Annabella, Jessamine, and me. We'd stay up all night telling fortunes and pretending we could read Tarot cards. I always thought it was sort of a strange hobby for a mom, but I liked that she was a little different and weird sometimes. She wasn't always that way, and the older we got, the more those weirdo days faded. Then she started trying to mold me into the perfect daughter, when I would've much preferred being the weirdo girl who learned how to read palms and Tarot cards. And then she died and those weirdo days were nonexistent. And my dad, who wanted to allow me to be who I wanted to be, even though I didn't know who that was and still don't, was gone, too.

"I was in the hospital when I heard the news about my parents' deaths," I say quietly. "It was the last time I've been there, and I … I don't know. Going back there … I'd just rather not go, if I don't have to."

Sympathy fills his eyes when I look up at him. Or maybe it's empathy. Has Ridge lost someone, too?

"My dad died when I was six," he tells me, confirming my speculation. "He actually worked in the organization and died on the job. I was at the hospital when I found out. I hate going there, too." A shaky sigh leaves his lips. "Unfortunately, my mom's a nurse, so I don't always get a choice."

"I'm sorry." I scoot to the very edge of the bed, lean forward, and give him a hug.

At first, his muscles wind up tightly, and I worry I've crossed some sort of line. But then he unstiffens and hugs me back, although he seems a bit uncomfortable.

"Okay, what'd I miss?" Wilder's voice sails from over my shoulder.

Ridge jerks away from me, as if he's done something wrong. He moves so quickly I start to face dive off the bed.

"Crap," Ridge mutters as he scrambles to catch me.

His arms envelope my waist right before I eat a mouthful of carpet. As he struggles to rebalance me, he loses his grip and I tumble forward, my face landing right in his crotch area.

My cheeks flame with heat as I push back and plant my ass back on the bed. The only thing that makes the awkward moment easier to handle is that Ridge's embarrassment seems equivalent, if not worse, than mine.

"Wow, Ridge. I mean, I know you suck when it comes to girls, but that was the least smooth move I've ever seen," Wilder says in a teasing tone. "And if you want a girl to put her face near your dic—"

"Don't finish that sentence," Ridge interrupts him, his voice loud, his cheeks bright red. "Or, I swear to God, the next time your computer crashes, I won't fix it."

"Oh, fine. Ruin my fun." Wilder wanders into the room and hands me the plate of food he's carrying, along with a cup. "Your Highness, here's your meal."

I giggle as I take the plate and cup from him. "Thank you."

He grins then plops down on the bed next to me, sitting close enough that our shoulders touch. "It's the healthiest meal I've ever made. It even has all four food groups. Well, that is, if you count chips and juice as the fruits and vegetables."

"It looks good," I say, fully meaning it. Sure, it's just a ham sandwich, some chips, and a glass of juice, but I'm so hungry right now I could eat almost anything and be happy about it. Besides, it's not every day a guy makes me something to eat.

I must be starving or something because, when I take a bite, it seriously seems like the best dang sandwich I've ever tasted.

"This is really, *really* good."

"Good. I'm glad." Wilder winks at me then claps his hands together and fixes his attention on Ridge. "Okay, so what's next?"

Ridge adjusts his glasses. "Well, right now I'm keeping an eye on Benton, Xavier, and Jackson. But we're all supposed to be on call in case they need backup."

"Why? Are they doing something dangerous?" I ask before popping a chip into my mouth.

Ridge and Wilder trade a silent look, and then they both shake their heads.

"Nah, it's just a protocol mission," Wilder says, but I get the impression he's lying.

"What's a protocol mission?" I ask, picking off the crust on the sandwich.

"It means it's a simple, standard mission." Wilder twists to face me, bringing his knee onto the bed. "Like, for instance, if we just have to go talk to someone or check up on something. It basically means nothing major will happen. In fact, we usually don't bring all our weapons on those kinds of missions."

"So, the thing with Axel wasn't a protocol mission?" I take a bite of the sandwich.

Wilder shakes his head. "Definitely not. In fact, that's not even considered a mission since it was completely unplanned."

"What's something like that called?" I ask, curious about the details of their world.

"Getting fucked in the ass," he replies.

"Oh." Heat rushes to my cheeks.

"You're cute when you blush," Wilder remarks, skimming his finger across my cheekbone. Then a musing smile tugs at his lips. "You know what? I think I'm going to call you Pink Cheeks from now on."

"Please don't," I beg, my cheeks heating up even more.

"Why not?" He juts out his lip. "Jackson said you let him call you Cute Girl."

"He decided to call me that all on his own," I explain through a grimace.

"So? What's the difference?" he asks, completely amused with himself. "They're both just nicknames."

"Because Pink Cheeks is a ridiculous nickname," Jett's voice floats from the doorway, startling the three of us and making us jump.

He's wearing a plaid shirt with the sleeves pushed up, a worn pair of jeans, and socks cover his feet. His shaggy brown hair is a mess, and his eyes are a little bloodshot, so I wonder if he's stoned.

"It'd be like me calling you Blue Balls," he tells Wilder with a dopey grin.

Wilder narrows his eyes at Jett. "That's not even remotely close to the same thing."

"Sure it is." He sneaks me a mischievous look I don't fully understand, and then grins at Wilder. "And if you nickname Zhara Pink Cheeks, then I'll make sure everyone starts calling you Blue Balls."

"Why? You suffer from it more than I do," Wilder quips. "So, it's probably more fitting for you."

While Jett and Wilder continue to argue about who should be called Blue Balls, Ridge offers me an apologetic look.

"I'm sorry," he says. "The organization tried to teach us manners, but not all of us passed."

"They're fine," I tell him. "I grew up with two brothers, so I know how guys can be sometimes." Although, I never heard my brothers try to nickname each other Blue Balls.

"Hey, we have manners." Jett walks over and jumps onto the bed, landing on his stomach behind me and making the mattress bounce. Then he rolls onto his side, props onto his elbow, and rests his chin on his hand. "We just choose not to use them all the time."

Ridge rolls his eyes. "Trust me; I know."

Wilder and Jett exchange a look then Wilder turns to Ridge.

"Of course you do," Wilder says. "Because you know everything."

Instead of getting upset, Ridge grins. "That might be the most accurate thing you've ever said."

"So, you're admitting you're a little know-it-all?" Jett mockingly gasps. "In front of Zhara?"

Ridge gives Jett a tolerant look. "I never said I was a know-it-all."

"But you're not denying it either," Jett quips, then I feel him tangle his fingers through my hair.

I stiffen as he repeats the movement again and again.

"Your hair's so soft," he states, combing his fingers through my hair again. "Have you ever wondered why?"

"Why my hair's soft?" I ask, sounding a little dazed. But I can't help it. What he's doing feels so good, like a lovely, little head massage.

"Yeah." Jett slowly combs his fingers from the top of

my scalp all the way to the ends of my hair. "I wonder if it's your shampoo. Or if your hair is just naturally soft."

Wilder twists around to look at Jett. "Seriously, man, how much have you smoked today?"

Jett considers it for a lengthy amount of time. "Not too much."

"Well, FYI, you're scaring Zhara with your stoner talk," Wilder says. "And the hair combing."

"He's fine," I tell Wilder. "My brother used to smoke pot when he was in high school, so I've heard stoner talk."

"But have you ever had a guy comb his fingers through your hair without your permission?" Wilder asks me, then blasts Jett with a dirty look.

"It's fine." If I was braver, I'd admit it feels good.

Wilder eyes me over suspiciously while Jett kneels up behind me.

"I think she likes my hair combing." Jett sweeps my hair to the side then lines his fingers along my shoulders. "I give great massages, too." He begins lightly working his fingers into my muscles.

It feels like I should tell him to stop, but it feels too good.

Wilder looks irritated, while Ridge seems a bit uncomfortable.

Beep. Beep. Beep.

"Crap," Ridge mutters, and Jett's fingers stop moving.

"What is it?" Wilder asks, lowering his feet to the floor.

Ridge shrugs. "It's nothing. The system's just being weird today." But when he briefly glances up at Wilder, a hint of worry flickers in his eyes.

Without saying a word, Wilder gets up and walks out of the room while Ridge begins typing like a madman on his computer.

Jett moves out from behind me, stands, and then offers me his hand. "Hey, do you want to take a shower? I'm sure you probably want to wash the night off or whatever the hell that saying is."

Taking a shower is the last thing on my mind, but I have an unsettling feeling they're trying to get me out of the room. So, not wanting to be a pain in the butt, I nod and take his hand.

He pulls me to my feet and guides me out of the room, but not before I hear Ridge's computer start beeping rapidly.

No one explains what the beeping is. And while Ridge said it was just a system malfunction, with how tense everyone got, I wonder if there's more to it. But I'm not brave enough to press for the truth. Besides, it might not even be any of my business. I mean, sure, they said I'm part of their team, but I haven't even done any training yet.

After Jett leads me out of the room, he steers me to a closed door at the end of the hallway.

"Here's the bathroom," he says, opening it.

"Yeah, I know," I tell him, remembering the last time I was in Benton's bathroom.

"You've been in Benton's place before?"

"Yeah, at the party he threw Friday night. The one where he had me pretend to be his girlfriend."

"Oh yeah. I forgot about that."

I nod my head at the bathroom doorway. "We also got locked in there for a while."

He eyes me over curiously. "In the bathroom? Together?"

"It was an accident," I quickly explain. "There was an incident with my shirt. It flew out the window, and I …" And now I'm stupidly babbling.

Face palm.

Jett rubs his hand across his mouth, probably to hide a smile. "So, you lost a shirt?"

"Not on purpose."

"Of course not. No one ever loses anything on purpose."

"That's not true. Alexis, my sister, used to lose her homework on purpose all the time."

"Alexis?" He pauses. "Alexis Baker is your sister?"

"My twin actually. Not identical, but that's probably pretty obvious." I pause, noticing how uncomfortable he's gotten. "Do you know her?"

"Not really." He scratches his neck with a pucker at his brow. When he notices me observing him, though, he simply offers me a small smile. "I'm going to go check with Ridge and make sure everything's okay. Holler if you need anything." Then he darts away so swiftly you'd think I had cooties.

And I'm left wondering what happened between my sister and Jett.

UM, YEAH, OF COURSE I CAN DANCE

I take a longer shower than I normally do, partially to clear my head and partially because the warm water feels good on my aching muscles. I know Ridge said devil's poison has no side effects, but with how achy my body is, I have to question if I react differently to the drug.

After I've scrubbed down my body and washed my hair, I step out of the shower to get dressed. Strangely, a crisp black shirt that looks about my size is sitting on top of my shorts and underwear. Weird, since I didn't hear anyone come in. The idea of one of the guys walking into the bathroom while I was showering makes my stomach somersault, and not necessarily in a bad way.

As the cold air nips at my skin, I hurriedly dry off, put the clothes on, and then search the drawers until I find a brush. I also stumble across some cologne and spray myself a few times since I don't have any deodorant. Between using Benton's body wash, shampoo, and cologne, I smell just like him.

"Hey," Jett greets me with a smile when I walk out into the living room.

The air smells like a mixture of strawberry air freshener and skunk, a lot like how Loki's bedroom used to smell back in his high school days. But the air is smokefree, so I'm guessing Jett smoked a bit ago then tried to mask the stench with a fruit-scented air freshener.

When I enter, his gaze lazily scrolls up and down my body, and a lopsided grin tugs at his lips. "I see you found the shirt I left you."

"Yeah, I did." I self-consciously tug at the hem of it. "But, how did you have a shirt my size?"

"It's actually Benton's. He has a whole drawer full of them."

I inch my way into the room. "Why does Benton have a whole drawer full of tiny shirts?"

Jett chuckles. "Because the damn fool didn't know how to use a washer and dryer properly and kept shrinking all his clothes. He went through, like, ten good shirts and pants before Wilder finally gave him a proper demonstration."

I giggle. "How old was he when this happened?"

"It was actually when he moved back to Honeyton.

Right after his …" He trails off and hastily clears his throat. "But yeah, anyway, apparently, he'd never touched a washer and dryer before. His mom always washed his clothes for him."

I've never heard the story of why Benton moved back to Honeyton or where his parents are. From what I understand, he's lived in this apartment alone for a while.

I take a seat beside Jett and tuck my hands underneath my legs. "Can I ask you a question about Benton?"

Wariness crosses his expression. "Sure."

"Can I ask …? I mean, do you know why he moved back to Honeyton? And if his parents moved with him?"

"His parents didn't move back with him." He restlessly drums his fingers on top of his knee. "As for the why, you'll have to talk to him about it. And I'd be careful when you do … Benton … He gets kind of uncomfortable talking about his past."

"I won't ask him then," I say. "I don't want to make him uncomfortable."

"No, you should ask him," he insists, fiddling with a lighter he picks up off the coffee table. "It's good for you to get to know everyone, especially since you're going to be working with us."

"So, then what's your story?" I ask bluntly then

instantly want to retract my statement. "Never mind. That was way too blunt."

"You need to quit being so polite." He playfully tugs on a strand of my damp hair then sighs heavily. "I can tell you my story, but it's not very pretty."

"Neither's mine," I tell him. "Or, well, the last few years of it anyway."

He offers me a sad smile. "Mine hasn't really been since the start. But that's okay. It's decent now." He rises to his feet and makes his way over to an iPod dock balanced on top of the flat screen. "Look, Zhara, I know I said you should get to know everyone, but I don't think telling you my entire story all at once is a good idea."

"Because it's too personal?"

"No, because it's too painful, and I don't want to make you sad." With his back turned to me, he picks up the iPod and begins scrolling through songs. "But, how about this? Every day that we hang out together, I'll tell you one thing about me, if you tell me one thing about you."

I nod. "That sounds doable."

"Good." He still doesn't turn around, seeming extremely fixated on the iPod. "So, here's one thing about me. I grew up without a family."

The crack that's permanently been in my heart since the day my parents died splits open even further. "Oh, my gosh. I'm so sorry."

He holds up a hand. "It's okay. No one died or anything. I just never had one."

"What do you mean?"

"I mean, my mom gave me away when I was about three years old, and I grew up in foster homes from then on."

My heart aches even more. Yes, my parents are dead, but at least they took care of me until then. "Jett, I'm so sorry."

"It's okay." He finally turns around. His eyes look a bit red, and I'm uncertain if he's tearing up or still stoned. "Everyone has their bad shit to deal with."

"Yeah, I know." I swallow hard. "My older brother's been raising me since I was fifteen."

He gives me an empathetic look. "Yeah, I know."

I wonder how he knows. If he heard the rumors around town or if maybe Alexis told him, since he seemed to know her. I want to ask him how he knows and why he seemed like he knew my sister, but then a song starts playing.

"Okay, enough sad talk." He sets the iPod down in the dock and faces me, rubbing his hands together. "So, I was instructed to give you some training lessons while everyone's gone."

"Wait. Everyone left?" I ask, suddenly realizing how empty the apartment seems.

He nods, making his way toward me. "Benton,

Xavier, and Jackson haven't come back yet, and Ridge and Wilder got called out on another job. They're actually not that far away, so they shouldn't be gone for too long. But I was instructed to keep an eye on you and give you some bad girl training."

"You want to give me bad girl training?" I ask, then glance at the clock. "At two o'clock in the morning?"

"Hey, the first rule of being a bad girl is that they don't worry about how late it is." He stops in front of me. "In fact, the later you stay up, the more bad you are."

I have a feeling he's teasing me but find myself smiling.

"Well, if that's the case, then I'm not very bad."

"Oh, but we're about to change that."

"By doing what?"

He offers me his hand. "By teaching you how to dance."

I shoot him a doubtful look. "That's your magical teaching lesson to make me a bad girl?"

"Yes," he replies simply. "All bad girls need to know how to dance."

"But I already know how to dance," I point out.

Now he's the one to give me a doubtful look. "Really?"

I nod. "I'm a cheerleader. Of course I can dance."

He considers this with an amused grin. "Maybe

that's true. But I don't really think the kind of dancing I'm talking about is the kind of dancing cheerleaders do."

"You mean, sexy dancing?" Warmth creeps across my cheeks, and I mentally curse myself for blushing over something so ridiculous.

Jett smiles amusedly. "You know what? You're cute when you blush."

It's always cute. Cute, cute, cute. I guess it might be time to accept my cute fate. And hey, it could be worse. He could be calling me Pink Cheeks.

"But anyway," I change the subject and Jett chuckles. "I know how to sexy dance."

His brow quirks upward. "Really?"

"Yes, really." I square my shoulders. "Taylor taught me."

"Taylor." He pulls a face. "I forgot you're friends with her."

"You don't like her?" Weird, since most guys do. Well, except Ridge and Benton.

"Well, I wouldn't necessarily say dislike so much as loath." He offers me a semi-apologetic look. "Sorry, I know she's your friend, but the girl does a lot of bitchy stuff to people who don't deserve it."

I frown, realizing the truth. "She wasn't always that way. Up until a few years ago, she was really nice."

"I'm not surprised."

"Really?"

He nods. "Of course. Otherwise, there's no way you would've become friends with her. Unless you're one of those firm believers that opposites attract."

"So, you think she's a bitch and I'm really … nice?" I'm unsure if I like that word more or less than *cute*.

"That's not a bad thing." He urges me to take his hand. "But right now, you're supposed to be being bad. So get your cute ass up and show me those sexy dance moves."

I can tell he still seems amused by the idea that I know how to sexy dance and that he doesn't fully believe me. While I don't blame him for doubting me, it makes my frustration tick, like when Benton wouldn't let me into the party.

"You don't think I can do it, huh?" I crook a brow.

"Of course I do." He presses his lips together, stifling a smile.

Squaring my shoulders, I plaster on a sassy grin. "Fine, I'll prove it."

I take his hand, but instead of letting him pull me up, I tug him forward while I jump to my feet. Then I wiggle my hand from his, line my palm to his chest, and push him down onto the sofa. When he gapes up at me, I put my hands on my hips and flash him another sassy smirk. On the inside, though, I give myself a mental high-five for pulling off the move. Sure, Taylor taught me how to sexy dance, but I never actually used the moves on a guy, so I'm a little shocked I managed to do it so smoothly.

Jett's shock shifts to interest. Reclining back on the sofa, he places his hands behind his head. "Okay, now I'm really interested in where this is going."

I smirk. "I bet you are. And maybe, if you're lucky, I'll show you." *What the heck!* Why are these words spilling out of my mouth? I'm such an idiot. *Think before you speak, Zhara. You're not Taylor!* "I'm so sorry. I don't know why I said that."

Jett shakes his head and motions for me to continue. "No, keep rolling with it. Don't lose the character."

Is he kidding me right now?

Apparently, he isn't, because he stares at me expectantly, waiting for me to continue.

I rack my brain for what Taylor would do next then frown at the mental image that pops into my mind. *Crap, I'm way in over my head.* Still, I have to try. Besides, sexy dancing in front of Jett can't be worse than getting tranquilized by a drug lord.

I hope, anyway.

Summoning a deep breath, I spin around while dragging my hands up my body. Once I do a full turn, I shimmy my hips, lower to the floor, then push back up. Jett watches my every move, his gaze transfixed. The longer I dance and the longer he continues to look at me with heat in his eyes, the braver I become.

I start to lose myself in the music, the rhythm, the sultry lyrics, the way I move my body. But as his eyes continue to heat, I'm thrown back to reality and start to panic.

"No, keep going," he encourages.

"I …" I don't know how to keep going when my heart is racing like this.

Sensing my panic, Jett gives me an encouraging smile. "Zhara, you're doing fine. Way better than I expected."

"Yeah?"

"Yeah." He wets his lips. "In fact, I think you were made for this."

"Sexy dancing?" I question with doubt.

"Sexy dancing. This job. Being a bad girl." The last part comes out more teasing and playful.

I start to relax, my muscles unwinding, when suddenly the music stops.

"Well, well, well, what do we have here?" a voice sails from across the room.

A voice that doesn't belong to any of the guys.

THE NOT-SO-FAMILIAR, YET
FAMILIAR INTRUDER

"Shit." Jett jumps to his feet and moves me around so I'm standing behind him. "How the fuck did you get in here without the alarms going off?"

"I have my ways." The guy pauses. "Who's that lovely, little thing hiding behind you?"

"That's none of your damn business," Jett snaps, sneaking his fingers into his back pocket for his phone.

"Don't you dare touch your phone," the guy warns, his booming voice making me shudder.

I hear a *click*, like a gun click, and Jett slowly moves his hands away from his back pocket and raises them to his sides.

My heart rate quickens so swiftly I worry I'm going to pass out, so I take a deep breath, trying to calm down. Still, I'm terrified. This is the second time I've been held at gunpoint in less than twenty-four hours. Is this going to become a thing when I'm with them? Will I quit if it is?

"Good. Now that I have your attention," the guy says, "I need you to answer a few questions for me, starting with you giving me the passcode to The Vault."

Jett lets out a low laugh. "I should've known that's what you're after. It's always the same with you rogues."

"I'm not the same as the rest of them," he growls. "I'm different."

Jett snorts a laugh. "Yeah, okay."

"*I am!*" the rogue screams, causing me to nearly jump out of my skin. "And besides, you don't even know what you're talking about. You don't even know what's really in there. You just believe everything your boss tells you, because you think that's how things are supposed to be. But believe me; if you knew the truth, you wouldn't be so trusting."

Jett's phone vibrates from inside his back pocket, the screen illuminating. I don't know what overcomes me, but I find myself moving to fish it out.

He momentarily tenses when I dip my hand inside his pocket, but then continues talking to the rogue.

"Like I'd trust a rogue." Jett laughs and shakes his head. "All you guys ever want is one thing—revenge. And you'll say just about anything to get it."

"Is that what they tell you?" The rogue lets out a snide laugh. "That we want revenge?"

When I get the phone all the way out of Jett's pocket, I hold my breath as I slowly swipe my finger over the screen. Crap, it's passcode protected.

"Of course that's what you want." Jett laughs. "And you want to know how I know this? Because I've heard the same story from rogues about nine thousand, four hundred, and fifty-seven times."

Okay, that was a really random number.

Or maybe it wasn't.

I type in nine, four, five, seven, and the screen unlocks.

Yes!

I quickly open his texts and type a message to Benton.

We need help. There's a rogue at the apartment that has Jett held up at gunpoint. Please hurry!

I hit *send* then hold my breath, waiting for a reply. But it never comes.

"And the stories are all the same," Jett continues. "Someone gets kicked out or gets pissed off and quits. You're all so angry at the organization for ruining your lives, when you were the ones who chose to enter."

"Chose to enter?" The hollow laugh the rogue

releases sends a chill down my spine. "Do you really believe that?"

"Of course I do," Jett replies. "No one forced me to join. I made the decision."

"Then you're really lucky. Or perhaps, if you'd said no, it would've been another story." He pauses for a lengthy amount of time then says, "The girl hiding behind you … I want to see her."

"Well, we don't always get what we want, do we?" Jett replies in a calm but firm tone.

"That wasn't a request," the man growls. "The girl is going to step out from behind you, or I'm going to make her."

Panicking, I quickly tuck the phone back into Jett's pocket. Then, with a few inhales and exhales, I step out from behind Jett.

For some reason, I pictured the rogue as an older man who'd spent too many days on the job. But shockingly, he looks around my age, with brown hair that reaches his shoulders, and a scar across his forehead. He's dressed in black cargo pants, a black T-shirt, and black boots.

He eyes me over thoroughly then pales, as if he's seen a ghost. "Zhara Baker?"

"You know her?" Jett looks at me for an explanation. "Do you know him?"

"I …" Puzzlement swirls through my mind as I

glance at the rogue then back at Jett. "I don't think so." This doesn't make sense. He doesn't look familiar, yet the feeling of familiarity presses against the back of my mind.

Who the hell am I?

Before I can delve too far into the strange wonderment of my identity, the sliding door to the deck bursts open. The rogue turns toward the door with the gun aimed in front of him as Jackson strolls in.

Jackson doesn't appear alarmed, and I soon find out why when Benton rushes in from seemingly out of nowhere, soundlessly moving like a freakin' ninja cat and Tasers the rogue in the back.

The gun falls from the rogue's hand, his eyes roll into the back of his head, and his body jerks as he collapses to the floor like a tree toppling over. Then he starts foaming at the mouth, his body thrashing all over the floor, and black lines start to weave across his flesh.

Shock whips through me, and I skitter back.

"Shit, he's one of them," Jett murmurs as Benton digs out a syringe from his pocket.

I gasp as he stabs the needle into the guy's neck. Seconds later, the man stills.

Question marks flood my mind. What the hell just happened? What were those lines that appeared on the guy's skin? And what did Jett mean by *he's one of them?*

"And … he's out," Jackson jokes. Then he surrenders

his hands in front of him when Benton shoots him a dirty look. "Sorry, but it's not my fault. The jokes just spill out."

Benton shakes his head as he pulls out a pair of handcuffs and straps them around the rogue's wrists.

"Hmm … I might know a way to help with that, Jacks," Jett muses, tapping his finger against his lip. "All you have to do is stop opening your mouth."

Jackson scowls at him. "Like you're one to talk."

Jett rolls his eyes. "I'm so not as bad as you—"

"That's enough," Benton cuts him off, his tone sharp.

The room grows so quiet I can hear the dripping of a faucet.

Benton gives Jackson and Jett a firm look before fixing his gaze on me, his eyes softening a smidgeon. "Are you okay?"

I nod. "I think so." But then I shake my head. "What were those lines on his arms?"

"Those were …" Benton trades a look with everyone then focuses back on me, his guard up. "There's some stuff I need to tell you, that I was planning on telling you when we got to the pit, but we never made it there, so …" He offers me his hand. "How about we go to my room, and I'll explain to you exactly what sort of mission we're working on?"

Hasn't he explained that already? Apparently not.

I frown, not taking his hand. "I thought you already told me."

"I did, but there're some parts that I haven't told you about yet because they're … a bit odd." Frowning, Benton lowers his hand and nods, indicating for me to follow him as he starts across the room.

"Wait," Jett says, and Benton pauses, glancing at him. Jett shifts his weight, his gaze bouncing from me then back to Benton. "The rogue … He knew Zhara."

Worry flashes across Benton's face. "Please tell me you're joking."

"I wish I could," Jett says. "But it's true."

Benton's worried look deepens as he looks at me. "Did you recognize him?"

"No … I mean … Well …" I press the heel of my hand to my forehead. "I don't know. He doesn't look familiar, but he feels familiar … That doesn't really make sense, though." I drop my hand to my side and free a trapped breath. "I had the same feeling with the guy who patted me down before we got into the car with Axel. And I have this memory of being in the car with my mom and that same guy … but I was really young at the time, so maybe I'm remembering wrong." I wait for someone to say something, but the room remains quiet. Worry creeps up inside me. "Is something wrong?"

Benton glances at Jackson then at Jett. Swallowing

hard, his gaze then collides with mine, a drop of fear residing within them.

"I think we need to talk now." He offers me his hand again.

Nerves bubble inside me at the sound of his fear-laced tone, so this time, I slip my fingers through his.

Jett and Jackson give me a look of pity as Benton leads me out of the room.

I have a feeling that whatever Benton is about to tell me is going to be bad.

Really, really bad.

SUPERPOWERS

After Benton takes me into his bedroom, he shuts the door. Without saying a word, he then shucks off his jacket, removes his holsters and guns, and kicks off his boots. Then he takes my hand in his and guides me toward the bed. He still doesn't speak as he helps me lie down. Then he tucks a pillow under my head and climbs into bed beside me so we're lying face to face.

"I have to tell you something," he says softly. "And it isn't going to be easy to hear."

I force down a shaky swallow. "Okay …?"

He rests his hand on my hip. "What I have to tell you is about your family." He blows out a stressed breath. "I don't think there's any easy way to say this, so I'm just going to say it." Another breath escapes his lips. "I'm pretty sure your family might have worked for an organization at one time."

Okay, so, I knew what he was going to say would probably shock me, but I didn't expect that.

"How do you know?" I ask shakily. "And wouldn't I know if they did?"

"Not necessarily." He traces circles along my hip with his fingertip. "A lot of times, parents choose not to tell their kids they work for the organization. At least, not until their kids are old enough to understand."

"But that doesn't make sense … When they died, we were old enough. At least Loki and Jessamine were … Oh, my gosh, what if they do know and no one ever told me!" Adrenaline courses through my veins. "What if everyone's been lying to me?"

"Zhara, calm down." His voice is gentle. "There's no reason to get worked up until we figure out exactly what's going on. For all I know, your parents could've quit a long time ago. Or maybe they were part of it before they were married. It's hard to say for sure."

"But, can you find out for sure?"

"I might be able to, but it's going to take some time." He glides his hand up my side and doesn't stop until he is cupping my cheek. "Until then, I need you not to worry. I'll—We'll take care of you. Nothing is going to happen to you. I won't let it."

"Am I not safe?"

"You are with us."

"What about when I go home?"

His gaze burns intensely into mine. "You'll be fine, I promise."

I hope I can trust him, but doubt weighs on my mind.

"You never explained to me what those lines were that appeared on the guy."

Benton swallows audibly. "It was a … a side effect from being a test subject at an experimental drug facility."

My lips part in shock. "Stuff like that exists?"

He gives a slight nod. "There's a lot of stuff in this world that people don't realize exists."

An uneven exhale slips from my lips. "What sort of stuff?"

"Stuff like what happened out there with the rogue." He gestures at the door then sighs and tugs his fingers through his hair. "The kind of drugs these facilities use on their subjects aren't your normal street drugs."

"So, like devil's poison?" I ask, chills slithering down my spine.

He gives a wary waver of his head. "Sort of. There're way worse stuff out there, though. Stuff that can make people do crazy, strange things." He huffs out a breath. "We've been trying to shut down these facilities for a while, but for every one we shut down, another seems to open." He scratches his brow. "The really shitty part is that most of the test subjects that we save are left dealing with side effects. Like that guy out there. Although, some of them are way worse off." His throat muscles work as he gulps.

"You make it seem like these tests make them like … bad or something."

"No, not bad. Now always anyway. Just … different."

"Like how?"

He gives a short, deciding pause. "I know this is going to sound crazy, but sometimes test subjects get … strange abilities."

"Like superpowers or something?" I question, expecting him to shake his head. So, when he hesitates, fear sweeps through me.

"I know this all sounds crazy," he says, "but when we get to the pit, I'll be able to explain it to you better. It's too risky saying too much out here."

My heart races in my chest. *This can't be real. I've got to be dreaming.*

"Why's that?"

"Because there're things there I can show you to prove what I'm saying, and there's not enough surveillance here for me to feel okay enough to say much more." He sinks into silence, grazing his thumb across my cheekbone. "You should try to get some sleep.

Tomorrow morning, I'll take you to the pit and explain everything with better detail, okay?"

Sleeping seems impossible. Not when my mind is so wired.

As my mind continues to race with questions, Benton leans in and places a soft kiss on my lips. "Close your eyes," he whispers, "and get some sleep."

I shake my head, but a few minutes later, I fall deeply into dreamland.

BENTON

I lie next to Zhara until she falls asleep, getting lost in the sound of her breathing, the way her lips are parted, how her eyelashes flutter occasionally. God, she's so fucking beautiful and doesn't even know it …

I blink, suddenly realizing how stupid I'm acting. Getting fixated on how some girl sleeps? Seriously, what the hell is wrong with me? I never get this caught up in a girl. So what if I kissed her twice? It was just part of my job. Well, the second kiss was …

Shaking my head at myself, I slip out of the room, leaving the door cracked open, and return to the living room where my team is waiting. The rogue has been picked up, so at least I can relax about that, and the rest of the team is back. But I have about a million other things to worry about, starting with …

"So, have you figured out how the rogue got in?" I ask Jett as I drop down onto the sofa.

Jett rubs his hand across the top of his head. "Honestly, I have no idea. The alarms didn't go off, so either he hacked the system or knew the passcode."

"There's no way he could've hacked the system," Ridge says. "My systems are un-hackable."

"But, how would he know the passcode?" Wilder questions. "The only way that's possible is if one of us told him."

They grow quiet, casting suspicious glances at each other, as if they actually believe for a second that one of us would betray the group. But deep down, we all know we can trust each other.

"Oh, knock it off. No one gave him the passcode." I recline back on the couch. "And Ridge, you're the best programmer we have, but you know as well as I do that no system is un-hackable."

Ridge opens his mouth to argue, but then thinks better of it and shuts up.

"That still doesn't explain how he got into the apartment without you hearing him, Jett," Xavier says while typing on his phone. "Unless you were too stoned."

"I wasn't too stoned," Jett says. "I was just a little preoccupied."

"With what?" Wilder asks, kicking his feet up onto the coffee table.

Jett shrugs. "Training Zhara, just like I was told to do."

Jackson eyes him over. "Training her how, exactly?"

Jett shrugs again. "Does it really matter?"

Before they can start arguing more, I clap my hands together. "All right, no more talking about this. We have bigger problems." I point at Jett. "The next time you're with Zhara, don't let yourself get so distracted. You're lucky she used your phone to text me for help."

He salutes me. "Yes, boss, sir. But just for the record, what she did was pretty badass. I mean, she just reached into my pocket and got out my phone without me even telling her to … She can think on her feet."

I nod, completely agreeing with him. Zhara is good with thinking on her feet, almost as if she belongs in this world, which might be closer to the truth than anyone realizes. "You're lucky she can."

"I know," Jett says, the humor in his eyes vanishing. "I'm sorry I fucked up."

"It's okay. We all do it sometimes. Just be more careful."

I turn to Ridge. "Okay, now for the next thing … I need you to do a favor for me."

He nods. "Sure. What's up?"

I hesitate, knowing he isn't going to like my request. "I need you to hack into the Shadow Files and see if you can access the list of names of all the people who have been rescued from all the Drug Tunnel Experiment Facilities the agency has shut down."

Ridge blinks at me, taken aback. "Those files are in the locked section. Do you know how much trouble I can get in if I get caught trying to access them?"

"Then don't get caught." I massage my temples with my fingertips, feeling a headache coming on. "Please, just do this, Ridge. It's important."

"Why?" he asks. "Because, if I'm going to hack into files that could potentially get me locked up, I'd at least like to know why I'm doing it."

I exchange a look with Xavier and Jackson, and then look back at Ridge. "Tonight was a setup. There was no Taylor. No weird cab driver. Taylor never sent any of those texts. She doesn't even have a clue what's going on."

"Then, how did this person text Zhara from Taylor's phone?" Jett asks.

"He bounced a signal from Taylor's phone," Ridge guesses, and I nod. "But why? And who was it?"

"Does the name Riverson Stellman ring a bell?" I ask.

Ridge's eyes widen. "The man who runs some of the Drug Tunnel Experiment Facilities?"

"Not just runs. *Created*," I remind him.

We've all heard the name Riverson Stellman. Many, many times, in fact, while we were test subjects. And, while we never actually saw the man, he was a rumor amongst everyone, the name thrown out every time someone wanted to instill fear in us.

"Holy shit," Jett breathes. "And you actually talked to him?"

"Only for a second," I say, shivering as I recall the memory of what it felt like to be face-to-face with the man who was the cause of a horrible, scarring, tainted time in my life. Although, calling him a man might be a stretch. "Then he took off. We tried to chase him down, but we lost him in the underground tunnels."

Jett shakes his head, stunned.

"Wait. Why did he text Zhara?" Ridge asks. "That doesn't make sense."

"Well, from what Riverson told us before he took off, it kind of does," I say. "Because, according to him, Zhara is a test patient from one of his old facilities. And not just one he created but ran personally."

Our gazes move to my bedroom door.

If what Riverson said is true, Zhara wasn't just a test subject at a drug facility like us, but a test subject at the most notorious experimental drug facility ever created. Most of the people who were rescued from there died right away from the damage the drugs did to their bodies. And the ones who lived turned into ... well, monsters.

Well, not all of them. We know of one that is completely okay, but only because he's in our group.

"It doesn't make sense," Jett mutters. "Zhara's too sweet."

He's right. But still, I can't figure out why Riverson would lie about something like that.

One thing's for sure; if it's true, then Zhara's life has been nothing but an illusion.

"Not every single test subject was bad," I remind him with a pressing look.

We grow quiet then and I make a silent vow to myself.

I'm going to get to the bottom of this, I vow to myself, *for bringing Zhara into this mess.*

Just like I'm going to protect Zhara, no matter what it takes.

But then my phone rings with a call that reminds me that I may not have as control over things as I want to.

There've been a couple of times in my life where I felt like I was about to watch someone break apart. Once was with my sister and the other time was with Jackson. Both times I wanted to help, but couldn't figure out what to do. So, I ended up silently watching them crumble into pieces. I still hate myself a little bit for not doing anything to help them.

The problem is, when a person's life is falling apart, it's nearly impossible to stop it. Perhaps that's why I don't want to tell Zhara what I just found out about her sister.

"We have a problem." I sit down in the sofa across from Jett. The rest of the guys are gone on a mission and Zhara is still sleeping in my bedroom. "And it has to do with Zhara."

He groans. "God, I don't think I can take much

more of this. No, scratch that. Fuck what I can't take. I'm just worried Zhara won't be able to deal with another problem. And we haven't even told her about your theory that she might have been a test subject."

"Actually, it's not about Zhara—it just concerns her." I sigh heavily. "It has to do with her sister."

Worry flashes in Jett's eyes. "Which one?"

"Alexis," I say and Jett squirms. "What's up? Do you not like Alexis or something?"

"No, it's not that."

"Then what is it? Because you look like something's bugging you."

"It's nothing." He waves me off. "So what's the problem?"

I can tell he's lying, but I don't have time to press. "You know Hacker Hearts Anonymous?"

He nods. "Of course I do. They're one of the most infamous hacker groups."

"Well, I got a lead that they might be getting ready to target Alexis."

He looks taken aback. "You mean, they're going to hack her?"

"I don't know the exact details yet," I say. "But I don't think they're planning on hacking her… They're up to something else."

Worry floods his eyes. "We need to warn her."

I completely agree with him. I may not know

Alexis, but she's Zhara's twin sister. If anything happened to her, it'd crush Zhara. And I'm not sure if Zhara can endure anymore crushing. Sure, she's strong, but the girl has dealt with too much shit the last few days.

"I think we should assign her some bodyguards," I say. "Until we can figure out what Hacker Hearts Anonymous is up to."

"But we're already short on people," Jett reminds me, giving a pressing glance around the nearly empty room.

"I'm not talking about one of us."

"Then who are you thinking?"

I hesitate, unsure how he's going to take what I'm about to say. "I think maybe we should call up our old team members."

Jett's brows rise. "You want to call West, Steel, and Ellis? Seriously?"

Letting out a deafening breath, I recline back in the sofa. "Look, I know we had a falling out due to a matter of different opinions, but they're one of the best teams out there. And they're trustworthy. Besides, if I'm remembering correctly, Alexis is friends with West, which might make it easier for her to get over the shock that undercover detective organizations exist."

Jett appears reluctant, probably over his anger he's been holding onto over West, Steel, and Ellis forming another team. But then his gaze wanders to my bedroom door and he sighs. "Fine, give them a call."

Nodding, I get to my feet and dial West's number, but his phone has been disconnected. Great. Tracking down a phone number for a member of the organization can be a pain in the ass and can take up to days. I don't have days. I need the phone number ASAP.

So, I dial Ridge's number, crossing my fingers he'll be able to hack into the organization's phone number files before the Hacker Hearts Anonymous finds Alexis.

Ridge isn't having very much luck with tracking down West's phone number. We tried Ellis and Steel's too, but they must have listed their phones as private, which makes them even harder to track down.

Seeing no other choice, I head into the bedroom to talk to Zhara and ask her to call Alexis. Although, I hate putting this on Zhara's shoulders. But if something happened to Alexis that I could've stopped, she'd never forgive me.

When I enter my room, she's awake and sitting up in the bed. She looks exhausted with dark circles underneath her eyes, her hair is a tangled mess, and she doesn't have a drop of makeup on. Still, she's gorgeous. And cute, no matter how much she hates that word.

"Hey," I say as I take a seat on the edge of the bed.

She flushes at my little nickname for her. "Hey… Sorry, I slept for so long and took over your bed."

"You're fine," I tell her. "I wouldn't have been sleeping anyway… I have too much work stuff going on."

"Is there anything I can help with?" she asks, tucking strands of her hair behind her ears. "Or do I still need to do more training before I can help?"

"Actually, you can help me with something."

She looks more than eager to help, and I'm starting to wonder if she likes this whole undercover thing. The thought makes me smile, but I worry about her getting hurt. Not just physically, but emotionally.

"I need you to call Alexis," I explain. "And see if you can get her to come here for a bit." While my plans are to have West, Ellis, and Steel keep an eye on her, I can't make that happen until I get a hold of them.

Her back stiffens. "Why? Is she in trouble?"

"Not yet." I take her hand to try to calm her down and then give her a quick recap of what's going on with Alexis, how we got information that some hackers were going after her.

By the time I'm finished, she's on the verge of freaking out.

"You don't know why these hackers are going after her?" she asks, worriedly biting her fingernails.

"Not yet. But I promise I will. And once we get a hold of West, Steel, or Ellis, we'll have them keep an eye on her and make sure she's safe."

Zhara nods, getting a funny look on her face. "I can't believe West is part of the organization. I've known him for forever." She grabs her phone out of her pocket then stares at the screen. "Any suggestions on what I should say to Alexis?"

"Why don't you call her and then hand the phone to me," I suggest, moving up beside her.

Nodding, she dials Alexis's number. Then she waits. And waits. And waits.

"She's not answering." She hangs up. "Let me send her a text to call me." She types in a message and we wait for a reply.

But after five minutes of silence, I start to worry that we might be too late. That perhaps Hacker Hearts Anonymous already found Alexis.

I keep trying to get a hold of West, refusing to give up, and finally he answers.

"Hello?"

"Hey," I say in relief.

"Benton? What's up man?" West asks, sounding a bit confused.

I get his confusion. He hasn't heard from me or my team members in quite a while, ever since they formed their own group. They didn't leave the group because they were pissed off or anything. They just decided they work better together as a trio.

"I actually need to ask you for a favor." I get straight to the point.

"Okay," he replies, lost, probably because I don't ask for favors very often.

"It's about your friend Alexis Baker," I explain. "She might be in trouble."

"I know," he tells me. "She actually is... Or was in trouble already. But she's at my place right now and safe."

"Let me guess, Hacker Hearts Anonymous?"

"Yep, they tried to attack her about an hour ago. But how did you know that?"

"I got an anonymous tip. I'm not sure who sent it, but Zhara and I have been trying to get ahold of Alexis all day to warn her. And you. But you're a really hard person to track down."

"So are you," he points out. "All organization members are."

"Yeah, I know." I sigh exhaustedly. "It just sucks when there's an emergency."

"Yeah, it definitely does." He pauses. "Wait, what're

you doing with Zhara Baker? She's not part of the organization… Is she?"

"Yes and no." I sigh again. "Look, I can't really get into the details over the phone, but I just want to make sure that Alexis is okay and being taken care of."

"She's fine. And I plan on keeping an eye on her until I can figure out what's going on with Hacker Hearts Anonymous."

I start to relax. Well, a little bit anyway. "Good, that's a fucking relief. Zhara's been really worried."

"So she knows a lot about what's going on?"

"Yeah, but not a lot of people know she does, so I'd appreciate it if you'd keep the information on the lowdown."

"Of course," he says. "I get it."

"Good." I pause. "Can Zhara talk to Alexis? She's been trying to call her but she won't answer her phone."

"Right now Alexis is… asleep. She got tranquilized. But everything's okay. I swear. And I'll have her call Zhara as soon as she can."

I tense at the mention of her being tranquilized. "She's okay, though, right?"

"I swear she is. Trust me, if she wasn't, I wouldn't be here talking to you. I'd be beating the shit out of the person who hurt her."

"Good." I believe him too. West was never one for lying.

After I get off the phone, I head to tell Zhara what happened to Alexis. Well, most of it anyway. But I think I might keep the tranquilizer part to myself for now. She's already too stressed out as it is. And I've seen too many people break apart in this world from being overly stressed out. I've watched people crumble. Disappear completely. And I'll do everything in my power to protect Zhara from that part of this world.

I've been worried sick every since Benton told me Alexis was in trouble. I still can't believe she's been dragged into this world and has hackers after her. Although, ever since my parents passed away, Alexis has been awfully secretive about where she goes when she leaves the house. Could she have known about this world the entire time? Did she do something to piss these Hackers off?

I frown, knowing the answer could be yes.

But that's not the only thing that took me off guard about the situation. I can't believe West is involved in the organization. Alexis has been friends with West for years. I've known West for years.

This is so weird.

How did I not know this?

"Hey, can I come in?" Benton asks, poking his head into the room.

I nod. "Of course."

He walks in and takes a seat beside me, seeming a tad bit squirrely. "So I got a hold of West."

Worry rushes through me. "Is she okay?"

He nods. "She is. They got to her in time and West and his team are going to keep an eye on her."

Relief washes over me. "Is there some way I can get a hold of her? Because she still won't answer my texts."

"She's probably busy with all of this shit going on." He pauses, mulling over something. "I'll tell you what. How about I drive you to the training pit to do some training and then we'll stop at West's on the way back so you can talk to her?"

I nod, letting out a breath I didn't even realize I was holding. While Alexis and I may fight, I don't know what I'd do if anything bad happened to her.

"Thanks, Benton." Then, acting on pure instinct, I lean in and give him a hug. "For everything."

He momentarily tenses but almost instantly hugs me back. When we finally pull away, he lightly brushes his lips against mine. The contact sends a shudder through my body and I blush, knowing he felt it.

A smile rises his lips as he leans forward and touches his lips to mine. Then he gets to his feet and offers me his hand.

"You ready for this?" he teases. "Because things might get a little intense."

I nod as I take his hand. "I trust you."

For a moment, I swear he flinches. But then his smile returns, he pulls me to my feet, and steers me toward the front door. I follow him easily, hoping upon hoping, I'm not making a mistake.

On our way out, Xavier walks in with a stack of papers. He frowns when his eyes land on me, grumbles something under his breath, a reminder of how much he likes me for reasons that are still unknown.

"Before you head out, we need to fill out some paper work," he tells Benton, setting the papers down on the counter.

Benton gives me an apologetic look. "Guess we're not quite heading to the training pit yet."

I relax a smidgeon, suddenly aware of how nervous I'd been about going. "That's fine."

"You seemed almost relieved by that?" he says with a hint of amusement.

I shake my head but then shrug. "I'm just a little nervous about going."

"You'll be fine," he assures me. "You've done great so far."

Xavier rolls his eyes, but Benton doesn't see him.

Then he picks up the papers he just set down. "I'm going to work on these in the spare bedroom." While he doesn't say it, I can almost hear a silent, *away from her*, at the end of his remark.

Benton sighs then follows after Xavier as he walks away. "I'll be done in a bit." He stuffs his hands into his pockets. "Why don't you get something to eat, okay?"

I nod then watch him walk out of the room with Xavier, the silence immediately making me uneasy.

I suddenly realize how chaotic everything has been over the last couple of days and how I haven't been alone much. As much as I've never minded not being alone, it bothers me a bit now. And that has me worried because eventually everything is going to go back to normal...

Right?

I'm not so sure.

I'm not sure about anything anymore.

YOU CAN ALWAYS EAT MY CEREAL IF YOU REALLY WANT TO.

While Benton and Xavier work on paperwork, I sit on in the living room, giving them space and eating some breakfast. I'm sitting in front of the television with a bowl of cereal on my lap. I feel exhausted, confused, and worried. Worried about myself, the guys. But most of all I'm worried about Alexis. Benton said she was okay, that West and two other guys from the organization are keeping an eye on her, I still haven't been able to get a hold of her. Until I see her, until I know for sure that she's okay, I don't think I'll be able to settle down.

I bounce my knee restlessly until Benton's bedroom door swings open and Benton strolls out.

He greets me with a smile. "Hey. You about ready to go?"

I absentmindedly stir the cereal. "To the training pit?"

Benton nods, moving to the side as Xavier exits the bedroom. Nothing appears different from when they first went into the bedroom, but for some reason I thought it would. I'm not sure why. Maybe because of all the chaos that's been going on?

Although, some slight things have changed with Benton's attire. He's still wearing the same jeans and black t-shirt he had on, but he now has on a hooded jacket. Since the temperature is at least eighty something degrees outside, I'm betting he has a gun hidden underneath the jacket.

But Xavier looks exactly the same as he did before he went into the room, sporting black jeans, a black shirt, and the black leather jacket that he wears almost all the time.

When he steps out of the room, his gaze locks with mine. Like always, he scowls. Benton discreetly jabs Xavier in the side and the scowl on Xavier's face fades into a neutral expression.

With a sigh, Benton crosses the room toward me. "Did you get enough to eat?"

I glance down at the bowl on my lap, half full of cereal and milk. "Yeah, I did. Thanks for letting me eat some of your cereal."

Xavier's lip twitches for some reason.

Benton tracks my gaze then frowns. "Is that your first bowl?"

I nod. "I don't feel very hungry. I think it's my nerves or something."

Benton crouches down in front of me, carrying my gaze. "What're you nervous about? What's going on with your sister? Or going to the pit?"

I shrug, watching the cereal go round and round as I stir the spoon through the milk. "All of that and I'm wondering what my mom was doing with a man like Axel. I know you said you think my family might've worked for an organization, but that doesn't explain why she took me in the car with a guy who works for a drug lord."

"I know. But like I said, I'm going to look into it." A crease forms between Benton's brows as he thrums his fingers on the cushion beside me. "I think I need to find a way to look into your parent's files and see if they worked a case on Axel. That might help explain why your mom knew him and why he knew her."

"Can you do that?" I wonder, perking up a bit.

I may not be thrilled about my parents lying to me, but it'd be great if they were simply working a case with Axel and not working for Axel. I feel awful for thinking she would do something like that, but can't shake the thought.

Benton wavers. "I might be able to. I mean, those

kinds of files are hard to access. At least most are. But if Ridge could…" He trails off with hesitancy written all over his face. "You know what? I'll look into it. But I'm not going to tell you how I'm going to do it."

I stop stirring the cereal, my lip jutting out. "Why not?"

He chuckles, pushing my lip back into place with his fingertip. "Stop pouting. This isn't a big deal. I just think that the less you know, the less you can be held account-able for if we get caught."

My pout morphs into a frown. "Are you doing some-thing illegal?"

"Not necessarily illegal by ordinary laws," he insists. "But with the organization's laws, it's kind of in the grey area."

"Which means it's not completely illegal but we could get into trouble if the wrong person catches us," Xavier explains, sitting down on the sofa next to me and startling the living bejesus out of me.

I think it might be the first time he's spoken directly to me. Well, except for when we first met and he chal-lenged my reasons for joining the team.

"So maybe you shouldn't do it then," I say. "I don't want you guys getting into trouble."

Benton glances at Xavier and raises his brows, a trace of a smile playing on his lips. Xavier shakes his head in annoyance. But I can't tell if his annoyance is aimed at Benton or me.

"We won't get into trouble," Xavier attempts to reassure me, although he doesn't sound too thrilled about it.

"Are you sure?" I ask him. "Because you don't sound too sure."

"Yes, I'm sure." Xavier stretches his arm across the back of the sofa. "We've done a lot of stuff that's considered in the grey area of the laws and we haven't gotten caught yet."

I set the bowl of cereal down on the end table. "But technically everyone can say that until they do something that gets them caught."

"Today's not the day we're going to get caught. Not over something as easy as this. We're too good," Xavier says. Then he reaches around me, collects the bowl of cereal, and sets it down on my lap. "Now eat up. It's going to be an exhausting day. Besides, you didn't eat most of the marshmallows, which is basically the only reason I buy the cereal."

Crap. I ate his cereal?

While most of the guys probably wouldn't mind, Xavier seems like the sort of guy who would care.

"Oh, I didn't know this was your cereal. Benton just said to help myself and this is my favorite kind," I apologize then take a bite. "I'm sorry. I'll make sure to eat every last drop."

Xavier trades a look with Benton, whose eyes glitter with amusement. Then Xavier sighs and redirects his attention back to me.

"It's fine," he mutters, standing to his feet. "You can always eat my cereal if you really want to."

I have no clue why, but his remark seems like a peace offering. If only I knew why he needed to offer peace with me to begin with. I guess it doesn't really matter, though. At least he's acting nicer to me.

"Thanks," I tell him then stuff another spoonful into my mouth.

He nods then heads for the door. "I'm going to go do a quick check of the area," he calls over his shoulder to Benton. "Text me when you guys are ready to go."

Benton nods and Xavier walks out of the apartment.

"He's going to the training pit with us?" I ask, trying to hide my worry.

Benton nods, fixing his gaze on me as he sits down on the edge of the coffee table in front of me. His knees touch mine as he rests back on his hands. "I promise he'll be nice, though."

"He's not being mean," I say. When Benton lifts his brows in speculation, I sigh. "Well, he wasn't just barely. But it's okay that he was before. If he doesn't want to like me, he doesn't have to. This is his world, not mine."

"That's not what his pissy attitude is about. Honestly, it doesn't really have anything to do with you."

"Then what does it have to do with?"

"That's not really my story to tell."

"Oh, okay." The guys have said that a lot to me, but Jett and Ridge did tell me a tiny piece of their sad pasts. In a strange way, it makes me feel connected to them. But I highly doubt Xavier will ever tell me his story.

Benton gives my leg a gentle pat. "Now, eat up and if you're a good girl, we might just stop by your place and let you change."

I narrow my eyes at him. "Only good girls get to change their clothes, huh?"

"Well, usually bad girls just take off their clothes." He winks at me and my cheeks erupt with heat. "If you're up for that, though, I'm totally cool with it."

I roll my eyes, trying to play off the embarrassment. "Fine, I'll play good girl for a few minutes so I can go change into some clean clothes."

"Your call." He shrugs, amusement dancing in his eyes. "But I think I should remind you that you did say you wanted to be a bad girl."

"I never used the words 'bad girl.' I just didn't want to be Miss Goody Goody Two Good For Her Own Shoes."

"And you still want that?" he questions, studying me closely.

I deliberate for a beat or two before nodding. "I think so." I stuff another bite of cereal into my mouth then get up to get ready to go. "Besides, after everything that's happened, I'm not sure I can go back to being plain, boring, naïve Zhara."

It's true, too. Whether I want it to be or not, my life was forever changed the moment I agreed to enter this world.

QUESTIONABLE NEXT-DOOR NEIGHBORS

So, here's the thing about my Bad Boy Rebels... I mentally roll my eyes at myself. My Bad Boy Rebels? Seriously, what is wrong with me?

But anyway, back to my point. Here's the thing about the Bad Boy Rebels. They're all gorgeous in their own unique way. Take Benton for example. Everything about him screams sexy bad boy, from his dark hair that's styled messily on top and shaved on the sides, to his facial piercings and smoldering looks. And I'm definitely not the only girl who notices how attractive he is—although it took me until recently to admit I find him attractive. Taylor's noticed too. Most of the cheerleading squad have as well. Even the girl who lives in the apartment across from Benton notices is hotness.

"Hey, Benton," she greets him with a flirty smile as

Benton and I exit his apartment at the same time she's walking out of her place.

She looks a few years older than me, with long, blonde hair and a curvy body that's on full display, since she's only wearing a bikini.

He gives her a subtle chin nod, focused on locking up his place.

She eyes him over, her gaze lingering on his butt as she bites her lip. "So, I heard you're going to have a party again Friday night?" She drapes the towel she's holding over her shoulder, not once giving a glance in my direction. "I know I've only lived here for a couple of weeks, but it seems like you're the only guy in Honeyton who has parties."

Wait? Benton's having a party on Friday? Since when?

Wait? Why am I surprised? This is Benton, who's known for his parties. The concept just seems sort of strange now that I know he's working for an undercover program. I don't know why. It's not like undercover guys can't have parties.

"There's other parties going on all the time," Benton tells Neighbor Girl as he stuffs the keys into the pocket of his jeans. "You just need to know the right people to talk to. People are pretty discreet about parties around here."

She coils a strand of her hair around her finger while biting on her bottom lip. "Really? I wonder why."

"Because everyone knows everyone and if the wrong person finds out, then the cops get called and your party place is no more." His gaze flicks to me, a smile playing on his lips. "I don't blame them, though. Sometimes the people who look like narcs aren't and vice versa. So, it's better just to keep things on the low down and only invite people you trust."

I can't help but smile at the memory of when I stood on this very porch less than a week ago and Benton accused me of being a narc. Clearly, he doesn't think of me this way anymore. At least, I don't think he does since he's told me so many secrets about his and his friend's lives.

"Oh, I totally get that." The girl's gaze strays in my direction for the first time. "Although, I think sometimes you can look at a person and tell that they're a good little girl who doesn't ever get into trouble. Those are the girls you need to look out for, you know." Her eyes glitter with maliciousness, but when she fixes her focus back on Benton, her demeanor is sugary sweet. "But anyway, what time's your party at? I thought I heard someone else in the building say it was around eight. But I want to make sure I don't show up too early."

I may be clueless in the guy department, but I've spent enough time with Taylor to understand when a girl is hitting on a guy. And when a girl is annoyed with another girl who's hanging around a guy she's trying to flirt with. Normally, Taylor tries to squash those girls like bugs, especially when they fight back. I don't want to be squashed by Neighbor Girl, but I also don't want to stand here and allow her to give me dirty looks simply for breathing next to a guy she thinks is hot. The problem is I've never been that good at sticking up for myself. Well, except for that one time Benton wouldn't let me into his party. I'm not a fan of drama either and I have a feeling Neighbor Girl will cause drama if I open my mouth.

I rack my brain for a way to handle the situation while Benton remains quiet, his gaze wandering to me again. He studies me for a drum beat of a moment and for the life of me, I can't read his expression.

"Actually, I was thinking I might cancel my party." He returns his gaze back to Neighbor Girl.

If looks could kill, I'd be a dead girl standing. I don't know why she's blaming me for what Benton said. It' s not like I'm some sort of great puppet master, forcing him to tell her things she doesn't want to hear. I probably couldn't force a guy to say anything if I tried.

The girl hastily erases the off-with-Zhara's-head look on her face and smiles sweetly at Benton. "Really? Why?" She pouts out her lip. "I was so looking forward to it. I heard you throw awesome parties."

"Sorry, but too many people know about it," he says with a nonchalant shrug. "Too many people I don't know. And like I said, having a bunch of strangers knowing your party location isn't good when you live in a small, gossipy town."

"Are you just going to move the location?" She steps forward, batting her eyelashes at him. "You can totally tell me if you are. I'm completely trustworthy, I swear. And if you'll let me, I can prove it to you." She shifts her arms closer to her sides, while leaning forward. The move practically causes her cleavage to pop out of her tiny bikini top.

I may not be a bad girl, but my mind conjures up all sorts of ideas of how she wants to prove her trustworthiness to Benton. And none of the ideas sit very well with me. But I won't allow myself to get upset. Benton isn't my boyfriend. Just my fake boyfriend. He doesn't belong to me and I don't belong to him. In fact, no one besides a drug lord and his workers think we're together.

"Hmm…." Benton rubs his jawline.

My stomach churns. Is he considering her offer?

"What's your name again?" he asks Neighbor Girl.

Her flirty smile briefly falters. "Brook. Remember? We met while I was headed out to the pool last week. You told me about the party you were having that night, and I said I couldn't come because I was headed out of town later."

"Oh yeah. I completely forgot about that. Although, I don't remember actually inviting you to the party. I think you just saw me and my friend hauling a keg into my house and invited yourself." He reaches over and laces his fingers through mine, something Brook more than notices. "And, from what I can remember, I planned on not letting you in if you showed up."

Her eyes narrow at him. "Well, that's just fucking rude."

"Well, I'm sort of a fucking rude guy, Brook. And all the people I trust know that about me," he tells her unapologetically then lightly tugs on my arm as he turns for the stairs.

He doesn't say goodbye. Just starts down the stairs.

"You know that girl you're with is a little tattle tell, right?" she shouts out after us. "You should hear the stuff people say about her. So, you should probably ditch her if you don't want untrustworthy people around you."

Benton pauses, his body going ridged. "How do you even know who she is?"

"I heard your friends mention her name a few times while they were going in and out of your place." Brook shrugs, her lips curling into a malicious smirk. "If I were you, I'd start being careful about what you say around here. The walls are really thin and people can hear almost everything. Even secrets you don't want other people to hear." Her gaze lands on me before she pushes past us, purposefully shoving my shoulder hard. I stumble to the side as she stomps down the stairs, but manage to regain my balance before I crash into the wall.

As I watch her go, I question if she was directing her last statement at me. Could that be possible? Are Benton and the guys keeping stuff from me?

Benton makes no move to unglue his feet from the step, remaining still while eyeballing Brook as she storms further down the stairway. When she nears the second floor, about to disappear out of our sight, her towel falls off her shoulder. Cursing, she bends over to pick it up. Her swimsuit bottom slips down a little, so she's sporting a nice little plumber's crack, and the tattoo on her upper butt cheek is on full display. A tattoo that looks like my creepy new neighbor's.

What the heck?

My gaze is yanked back to Benton as a gradual breath eases from his lips.

"I think we might have another problem on our hands," he mumbles, shaking his head.

"Another one?" I ask, unsure whether to be shocked at this point or used to it.

He nods slowly, his gaze skating to me. Worry fills his eyes as his fingers thread through mine.

I open my mouth to ask him what's wrong and to tell him about the tattoo, but he gives a firm shake of his head.

Not here, he mouths. Just act natural.

I don't know what's going on, but I trust him enough to keep my lips zipped and pretend like nothing happened. I hope trusting him is the right thing to do. That he isn't keeping secrets from me like everyone else seems to be.

Benton stays quiet as we start down the stairwell, holding hands, and heading toward the apartment parking lot where his car is parked.

So many questions ping pong around in my brain, nearly driving me insane. I want to ask him who Brook is, why she seemed to be threatening Benton when she said the walls were thin, why he suddenly seems so uneasy, and why on earth Brook has the same tattoo as my new neighbor, Creepy Charles. Benton has told me to stay away from him, which makes me wonder if Charles isn't a normal guy.

I can't ask any questions now though, so I decide to busy myself with a normal conversation topic that will hopefully distract me from all the weirdness that just occurred.

"Have you heard anything about Alexis?" I ask, hoping he doesn't notice that my palm is starting to sweat in his hand.

The sun is up in the crystal blue sky and blaring heat down on Honeyton, making me wish I had my sunglasses and a tank top on.

Benton blinks, as if coming out of a daze, then checks his phone and shakes his head. "Not yet. But it's only been a few hours since everything went down. She's probably still trying to process everything."

I tuck a few strands of my tangled, wavy brown hair behind my ears. "But we're still going to see her after we go to the training pit, right?"

He nods. "I think it's going to help if you're there. It might help her cope with all of this better if she has someone she's close to who knows everything."

"I really don't think I'm going to be able to help her," I tell him sadly. When Benton shoots me a questioning look as we reach the bottom of the stair, I add, "Alexis and I used to be close, but then our parents died... And... Well, she changed while I stayed the same." I give a half shrug, but my heart aches at the brutal truth of what I'm about to say next. "We haven't gotten along since then."

"That sucks," he says as we hike down the sidewalk toward the carport. "Maybe this can help you guys grow close again, though."

"Yeah, maybe." But I'm a bit skeptical. While Alexis is my sister, sometimes I feel like she wishes I wasn't. That I'm only an annoyance to her. A reminder of another life she's trying to forget. I shield my eyes from the sunlight and glance at Benton. "Do you have any brothers or sisters?"

He stares ahead at the parking lot, the sunlight reflecting against the sudden pain filling his eyes. "I had a sister, but she died a while ago."

"Oh my Gosh, I'm so sorry, Benton." Knowing how hard it is to lose a loved one, my heart aches for him.

"It's part of the reason why I started working for the organization." He swallows hard, dazing off as we stop in front of his car. Then he quickly clears his throat. "But anyway, I think you should try to smooth things over with your sister. It'll be good for you to have someone to talk to who knows about the organizations." He busies himself with retrieving his car keys from his pocket, not meeting my gaze.

I stand at the front of the car, observing him as he fumbles to unlock the door. Whatever happened to his sister, had to be terrible. But what happened that made him join the organization? And how did he even find out about the organization?

Sensing he wants to change the subject, though, I refrain from asking him. Besides, Jett warned me that Benton doesn't like talking about his past.

"What if they do know?" I ask, pulling open the passenger side door.

Benton glances over the roof at me with a pucker at his brow. "Who knows what?"

"Loki, Jessamine, and Annabella. They're all older than me. Perhaps they knew more about what was going on, but just never said anything because my parents told them not to."

He wavers. "That could be a possibility but I highly doubt it. Like I said earlier, a lot of parents that work for the organization choose not to tell their kids until they're older. And sometimes they don't tell them at all."

"I know you said that, but what if one of my brothers or sisters knows something and can give us some answers. Then maybe you guys won't have to do any of that kinda, sorta, not quite illegal stuff you're planning on doing."

A hint of an amused smile graces his lips. "You're a sweet girl, Zhara. You really are." When I start to frown, he adds, "Don't take that the wrong way. I mean it as a compliment."

He ducks into the car, sliding into the driver's seat. I follow, slipping onto the warm leather of the passenger seat. We both close the doors then he twists in the seat to face me.

"Look, I know you want answers, but I think the best thing to do is let Ridge find as much as he can in the files about your parents. Then, if we can't find the answers, we need, we'll go talk to your brothers and sisters. But the files are a better option right now and probably will have more detailed information."

Even though I want to talk to my siblings and find out if they know, I get what he's saying.

"All right, I'll wait," I tell him. "I just hope you guys don't get into trouble."

He offers me a lopsided smile then reaches across the console and lightly tugs on a strand of my hair. "See, sweet."

My mouth dips to a pouty frown, which only makes Benton's grin broaden. Then his gaze travels in the direction of the window behind me and the smile goes *poof.* I turn to track his gaze, but his hand cups the back of my head, holding me in place. Before I can even comprehend what he's doing, he leans in to kiss me.

"Act natural," he whispers then his lips softly collide with mine.

I tense. *Act natural? Again? How is kissing him even acting natural? It's not like we kiss all the time? How is any of that natural! Seriously, acting natural is becoming complicated!*

But all of my questioning goes bye bye, see ya later, as Benton parts my lips with his tongue.

Unlike the first time we kissed, I'm not such a bundle of nerves. Am I nervous? Sure. But not enough to break the kiss. In fact, I'm sort of enjoying his warm lips against mine, an unexpected moan faltering from my lips.

Okay, maybe I'm enjoying this a lot.

"I love it when you make that sound," he whispers, his tone a mixture of amusement and something else I don't recognize, but it makes my stomach flutter with crazy, dazed butterflies.

Then he kisses me again, his fingers threading through my hair as he softly tugs on the strands, and forces my head to tilt back. His lips leave mine and travel downward, along my jawline, my throat, to the hollow of my neck. He pauses, breathing softly against my skin, before nipping and sucking a path toward my shoulder, slowly guiding my shirt over so his lips touch my bare skin. With every graze of his teeth, my heart turns more into a cracked out humming bird. By the time his mouth reaches my shoulder, goose bumps have sprouted across my skin and my entire body is trembling. But I'm not afraid. Well, sort of. Honestly, I'm partially afraid and partially excited.

"God, you're going to be the death of me," Benton mumbles as my body shudders again. "Maybe all of us."

"What?" I asked dazedly as he gently sucks on my collarbone.

Instead of answering, he kisses the side of my neck, right where my pulse is hammering, then pulls away.

I open my mouth to ask him what on earth was that

about, when someone raps on the window behind me. I nearly jolt out of my seat, whipping around to see who it is. But Benton places a hand on my thigh, stopping me. He mouths, *bad girl*, before withdrawing his hand.

Confusion tap dances in my mind until I peek over my shoulder. Then things—and by things, I mean all the kisses and biting that just happened between Benton and I—start to make sense. Because standing beside the passenger side door is none other than Tank and Ralpho.

They're about as intimidating as I remember, decked out in black pants, leather jackets, and combat boots. Sunglasses cover their eyes and brass knuckles bedazzle their knuckles. Okay, maybe bedazzle isn't the best word, but against the sunlight, the metal looks awfully sparkly.

"Just remain calm," Benton whispers, reaching for the door handle. "And stay in the car."

When I nod, he hops out and rounds the front of the car toward Tank and Ralpho.

"Gentlemen, to what do I owe yet another unexpected visit from you?" Benton asks, stuffing his hands into his pockets.

"Easy with the cocky tone," the shorter guy warns—I still haven't figured out which one is Tank and which one is Ralpho. "If Drake sends an unexpected visit on you, you don't question his motives."

Drake? Who's Drake?

"I'm not questioning our boss's motives, Ralpho," Benton assures him. "I was just curious why you stopped by. That's all."

I make a mental note that the shorter guy is Ralpho and the taller one must be Tank, and that Drake is probably their boss.

Tank and Ralpho glance at each other and Tank nods his head. A sly grin slowly rises on Ralpho's lips as he flits a glance at me. I can't see his eyes, but just having his attention zeroed in on me is very intimidating. So much so that I nearly dive into the backseat to escape it. But then I remember the words Benton mouthed to me before he got out of the car.

Bad girl.

I'm supposed to be acting like a bad girl. And a bad girl wouldn't dive into the backseat to hide from the gazes of two guys. No, she'd probably only dive into the backseat with two guys.

I blink at my dirty thought. Holy crap, where did that dirty thought come from?

My fingers wander to my neck and then my lips. *Maybe all this kissing is messing with my head?*

"We came here to give you invitations." Ralpho centers his gaze on Benton, the devious smile remaining on his face. "To Drake's Annual Undead Masquerade."

Undead Masquerade? That sounds… interesting. And seems to perk Benton up a tad.

"Really?" Benton asks, his brows raising toward his hairline. "I thought he didn't invite first years?"

"Apparently you and your friends have impressed him." A drop of disdain rings in Ralpho's tone. "I don't know why. I haven't seen you do anything that impressive. In fact, you guys have done nothing but shitty work since the day you started working with us."

"You know your boss wouldn't be saying we're doing a good job unless we were," Benton points out. "It's not his MO."

"No, it's not. Just like it's not his MO to invite a first year to the masquerade," Ralpho snaps. "And for a good reason. It takes time to trust people—more than a year."

Huh. Benton said something similar to Brook.

I guess trust is a big deal in the drug world and in the undercover detective world. Wish it was in my family.

I shake my head. *No, don't think about that right now!*

Shoving the thought aside, I concentrate on Benton, Tank, and Ralpho, wondering what happens at a masquerade party thrown by a drug lord and why the three of them are acting like it's a huge deal. It's just a party. Isn't it?

"I'm sorry you feel that way." Benton leans against

the passenger door, blocking my view of Ralpho. "But unfortunately, you don't get the final say. Drake does."

A beat of silence ticks by.

"Yeah, see, here's the thing," Ralpho says. "Our boss may have invited you, but he hired us to watch out for him, which means we make certain judgment calls without him."

"So you're saying you're taking back our invites?" Benton questions, slipping his hands into the back pockets of his jeans. "Because that doesn't seem like a very smart move on your part."

"We're not taking them back—we couldn't even if we wanted to." Ralpho gives a lengthy pause. "But, we are going to make sure you earn them."

The muscles in Benton's arms bulge as he stiffens. "Oh yeah. How?"

"By giving you a test," Ralpho says. Or more like sneers. "If you pass, I'll be happy to give you the invites. If you fail, I'm tearing the invites up."

"But that'd make Drake pissed off," Benton points out, giving him a pressing look. "At *you*."

"No, he'd be pissed off at you, since I plan on telling him you declined his invite." Ralpho lets out a dark laugh. "Don't worry, though. If you pass my test, I'll be more than happy to give you the invites. Plus, I'll throw in the added bonus of not dragging that pretty girl of yours out of the car."

Benton steps forward, removing his hands from his pockets. "Zhara isn't part of this so stay the hell away from her."

"I told you when I first met her that I wanted to talk to her on Monday. Today is Monday, so I get to talk to her." Ralpho slants to the side, lifts up his sunglasses, and winks at me.

I smash my lips together, unsure how to respond. Thankfully, Benton sidesteps and blocks me from Ralpho's view again.

"Tonight's when the meeting is taking place," Benton grits out. "It's not even noon yet. So, you have six more hours before you can talk to her."

"If I want to talk to her now, I'll talk to her now." Ralpho's demanding tone sends a shiver down my spine. "You don't give the orders."

Benton opens and flexes his hands. "No, I don't. But neither do you."

"I have more authority than you," Ralpho argues. "But don't worry, I'll give the girl a get out of jail free pass for the next six hours if you pass the test."

Benton's hands curl into fists. "And what's the test?"

"Oh, it's pretty simple," Ralpho insists, but the amusement lacing his voice suggests otherwise. "Well, it'll be if you've been telling me the truth about the girl."

My back goes rigid. *What has Benton told them about me?*

"What have I told you?" Benton's tone carries

caution. "Because I haven't told you anything about her really, other than she's dating me."

"I know," Ralpho says. "And while you insisted she was, I'm still not sure I buy it. So, I'm asking for more. You give it to me, I give you the invites and leave your girl alone until tonight. You fail, I tell Drake you decline the invites and I'm going to take one of your boys and have a nice, long *chat* with him."

Chills break out across my skin. No one has explained to me what chat means in the drug world, but I'm fairly positive it doesn't mean having a nice, long talk.

"How do you expect me to prove she's my girl-friend?" Again, Benton's tone is guarded.

"This isn't about proving anything. This is about passing a test." The low laugh that reverberates from Ralpho's lips as he leans to the side and catches my eye causes my stomach to ravel into knots.

I shiver. What kind of a test? A few ideas pop into my mind my mind. Scenarios I'm not ready for and that scare me.

Then a lump wedges in my throat. *If I don't do what they say, they might hurt one of the guys.*

"If you want a show, go to a strip club," Benton replies flatly. "Because, whatever you're thinking, isn't going to happen."

"You have no idea what I'm thinking, so don't make

assumptions," Ralpho retorts, looking highly entertained as he glances from me to Benton. "I'm not going to make you and her fuck in the car while we watch. I don't get my kicks off of other guys fucking women. I prefer doing it myself." He drags out a pause. "However, if I wanted you to, you'd have to, or else one of your boys would be," he brings his finger to his neck and drags it along his throat.

My pulse quickens and my stomach winds into even more knots as I realize the full meaning of the word *chat.*

"But like I said, I prefer fucking women, not watching other men fuck women." He lowers his hand from his throat. "So, for the test, all I want is for you to get your girl out of the car and give her another one of those passionate," he rolls his eyes, as if he thinks the word is stupid, "kisses you were giving her when we walked up. And then have one of your other guys do the same."

Benton gaps at him. "How the hell does is that a test?"

"Because I say it is. And if you pass, then I'll let this go." His eyes darken. "For now, anyway."

For now? Does that mean will have to prove more to him later? Because thinking about kissing two guys in front of Tank and Ralpho is already turning my stomach into an out of control bouncy house crammed with insane butterflies.

But no, there's no way Benton will ask me to do that... Will he?

"And then if you pass, you'll get your invites and we'll leave everyone alone until later tonight," Ralpho prattles on. "And then the girl can prove her trustworthiness."

Great. Now not only do I have to make out with two guys in front of two guys, but I have to prove my trustworthiness to a drug dealer.

I press my forehead to the window, the glass warm against my chilled skin. I want to help the guys—I really do—but my mind is spinning a million miles a minute and I can barely think straight.

I don't think I can do this.

"I still don't understand what the point is of having her kiss someone else," Benton says in a quiet but steady voice.

"You guys are always bragging about how close you are," Ralpho says with a smirk. "So we figured this would be a good way to prove if you're really telling the truth. Plus, it'll show how important Drake's approval is to you."

Benton shakes his head from side to side, tension rippling off him. "Look, I really want to pass the test, but right now, all my guys are out. Maybe later tonight we can do it."

"If your guys are all gone then who's that?" Ralpho

nods in the direction of the entrance to the apartment complex.

I rotate around in the seat to see who he nodded at. Then my heart goes from a galloping horse to a freakin' sprinting wild mustang.

Xavier is entering the parking lot, coming from who the heck knows where.

"He must've just got back," Benton mutters, his worried gaze skimming toward me and making my nerves double.

"Well, lucky for you, he did." Ralpho claps his hands together and the brass knuckles clank together, making an ear grating noise. "Now, get the girl out of the car so we can get this done."

Clenching his hands into fists, Benton twists toward me. Remorse radiates from his eyes as he reaches for the door handle and pulls the door open.

It'll be fine, he mouths then offers me his hand.

I want to believe him—I really do. And maybe if it were any of the other guys in place of Xavier, I might not be so nervous about doing this. But Xavier doesn't like me. He may have been nice to me this morning, but that doesn't mean he's going to be happy about being forced to kiss me and I'm not so sure I'm that thrilled to be kissing him either. I mean, two guys? I have to kiss two guys in a row?

I'm not sure I have that in me or that my nerves can handle it.

But, seeing no other choice than to trust Benton again, I place my hand in his and let him pull me to my feet. Then I hold my breath and wait for Xavier to reach us, hoping upon hoping that everything will turn out okay.

Because one of the guy's life might depend on it.

SWEET KISSES

My heart is an erratic mess as I stand beside Benton, waiting for Xavier to reach us. Xavier seems oblivious to the scene, his eyes glued to his phone as he crosses the parking lot. This makes my uneasiness go up a notch. He's walking straight into a dangerous mess and he's not even aware of it.

But when Xavier's gaze finds us, not an ounce of surprise flashes across his expression. I suddenly second guess my initial assumption and question if he either somehow knew Tank and Ralpho were here or that he's just really good at concealing his shock.

When Benton catches my gaze, he gives my hand a reassuring squeeze.

I realize three things right then and there. 1). Xavier knew Ralpho and Tank were here, maybe the entire time. And 2). The guys are pros at acting. And 3). I shouldn't doubt them when the situation looks hopeless.

Then a fourth thing occurs to me. That I'm actually going to kiss both of these guys while Ralpho and Tank watch.

How is this my life now?

I could always just run, but what kind of a person would that make me?

"Xavier, so glad you can join us." Ralpho throws a smirk in Xavier's direction. "It's actually perfect timing. I was just about to go find one of your boys and have a little chat with them. But, since you're here, you can spare one of them a talk. That is, if you pass the test."

Xavier's eyes momentarily drift toward Benton before landing back on Ralpho. "Oh yeah? A test, huh?" He doesn't sound surprised. Just mildly curious.

I have to wonder if he knows exactly what's going on, if Benton somehow informed him. But why would he show up if he knew he was going to have to kiss me? If he didn't, would Ralpho really track down one of the guys right this very moment and kill them? Yes. The answer has to be yes.

The realization of how dangerous these guys are sends a shiver coursing through my body. Not wanting Ralpho and Tank to notice my spastic behavior, I inch closer to Benton and he strokes his finger along the inside of my wrist.

"Yeah, a test." Ralpho seems irritated by Xavier's lack of worry. "You're going to prove to me and Tank right now where you're loyalty lies." His lips twist into a snide grin. "Personally, I don't think it's going to work. I think the girl's going to run off before it can happen." His dark gaze zeroes in on me and he wets his lips with his tongue. "She looks like too good of a girl to go through with this."

"Sometimes it's the good girls who are the naughty ones." Tank speaks for the first time pretty much since they showed up. He lifts off his glasses to get a good look at me, revealing a faint scar underneath his left eye. "Isn't that right, Zhara Baker?"

I gulp at his use of my last name and Benton's hand clamps down on mine.

Tank grins. "Yeah, I did a little research on you. Thought it was a good idea since you were running around with a bunch of guys who know a lot about my boss." His head angles to the side and his gaze bores into me. "I couldn't find much about you, though. So, either you're just a really good girl who never does anything, bad or someone wiped your records clean. But it doesn't make sense. I mean, supposedly you're dating Benton. but you haven't ever gotten into trouble, you graduated with honors, and no one in our circle has ever heard of you."

Well, at least no one recognizes my last name. That's

got to be a good sign that perhaps my mom wasn't working for Axel, right? Either that or she used an alias.

Tank stares at me expectantly, and I get the impression this is one of those moments where I'm supposed to say something. I just wish I knew what was the correct thing to say.

Do something, Zhara! Just say something sassy and snarky that will put them in their place. Be the Zhara that was sexy dancing in front of Jett, that told him maybe if he was lucky, you'd show him some more. Put that brief bad girl training to use.

Yep, even in a panicking situation, apparently my initial instinct is to go with what I've been taught. I've been trying to break the habit, but considering I'm completely clueless about being a bad girl, I can only go with what I've learned.

Summoning a deep breath, I let my lips part, still uncertain what I'm going to say.

"You think just because I'm smart, haven't been arrested, and some guys from your little drug circle haven't heard about me, that means I can't date guys like Benton? Sounds like you're not the smart ones." *Oh my gosh, why the freakin' heck did I just say that!*

I want to slap my hand across my mouth and retract every word. But when I'd tried to take back the sassy remark I made to Jett, he told me not to lose character. So, instead of backing out, I push onward and turn to Benton. Then, without looking at his expression—

because I'm sure he's freaking out, which is only going to make me freak out—I seal my lips to his.

Everything about what I've said and done up until this point has been carried out with utter confidence, despite my internal panicking. But as Benton's arm winds around my back and he deepens the kiss, my knees begin to wobble and my nerves slip through. Still, having kissed Benton before, I manage to keep my freaking out to a minimum. I worry, though, how I'm going to react when I have to kiss Xavier.

As more worry possesses me, I begin to kiss Benton quicker, almost in a frenzy. Benton is the perfect actor, going along with my crazy kissing, his tongue frantically tangling with mine. The longer we kiss, the more my legs tremble and all I can do is clutch onto him for dear life. Somewhere through the haziness fogging up my brain, I swear I hear Benton groan. Then his hands wander around my back and brush across my butt, which only makes my body shudder so badly I worry my knees are going to buckle. Before I collapse, he grips the back of my legs and picks me up. I tense, unsure what to do, but he helps me out and guides my legs around his waist.

The longer we kiss, the more I forget about my outside surroundings. I don't know how I manage to forget though, with Tank and Ralpho watching us, but somehow I do. I even forget that when Benton's lips leave mine, I have to seal my lips to another set of lips that belong to a guy who doesn't like me. Yes, it seems pretty crazy to forget about all of that, yet somewhere between Benton picking me up and kissing me for so long I can barely breathe, my mind tunes out everything else.

But the instant Benton breaks the kiss, reality douses over me like a cold shower.

"Are you okay?" Benton whispers quietly enough for only me to hear, his lips hovering a sliver of an inch away from mine.

I nod my head once, unable to form coherent words.

"Good. Just hang on for a little longer, okay?" He kisses me once more, a gentle graze across my lips before pulling away.

Taking the hint, I untangle my legs from him and lower my feet to the ground. I only allow myself one deep breath before I turn and approach Xavier. He carries my gaze as I walk toward him. Or more like wobble toward him. And while I'm the one who started the situation—who kissed Benton—I suddenly feel like Xavier's in control, as if a rope is wound around my wrists and he's pulling me toward him. Step by step, I move closer to him until I'm finally standing right in front of him. Then I tip my chin up to meet his eyes, which is strange, since I'm above average height. Xavier has to be tall. When did he get so tall? Has he been this tall the entire time? Have I somehow become one of those completely oblivious people?

I mentally smack myself in the forehead. Seriously, I'm about to kiss Xavier and all I can think about is how tall he is and that I've become oblivious.

Get your head in the game, Zhara!

Blinking from my thoughts, I focus on Xavier and his lips. I need to kiss him. But throwing myself at him isn't as easy as it was with Benton. I know Benton better. Know he doesn't entirely despise me.

As I stand there stupidly, my palms begin to sweat. I want to wipe them off on the sides of my shorts, but fear Tank and Ralpho will notice.

Just kiss him, you idiot! Do it!

I start to lean forward, but freeze. *I can't do this! I just can't!*

Xavier gives me a look, as if he's resisting an eye roll —like he expected me not to be able to follow through with this. That look is my weakness, the thing that sets a fire of fury off inside me.

He thinks I won't do it. That I'm a good girl. That he was right about me.

Before I can back out, I stand on my tiptoes and smash my lips against his. And when I say smash, I mean *smash*, our teeth clanking together so forcefully I swear my brain vibrates inside my skull. Xavier groans, either from the intensity of the kiss or the fact that I just about knocked his teeth out. My guess is the latter.

I don't pull away, though, gripping onto his shoulders and pressing my body against his. For the briefest second, he stands stiffly against me. I grow worried he isn't going to kiss me back. But a pounding of a heartbeat later, he takes over. And I mean *really* takes over.

Xavier is an intense kisser—that's the first thing I learn within the first second of our kiss. His tongue moves passionately against mine as he picks me up and backs us up toward the car, giving me hardly any time to get my legs wrapped around his waist. Still, I manage to before he presses me up against the side of the car. Then he deepens the kiss, his hands skimming across my waist, my sides, my shoulders before residing on the sides of my neck. He holds me gently, but firmly, which really makes no sense. Yet in my cloudy, overly kissed brain, it does.

Kissed. I'm getting kissed so much I can't even remember what it was like not to be kissed.

My mind and heart are soaring as I rush to keep up with his movements. When a groan slips from his lips, the kiss goes from wildly intense to frantically crazy and any attempt at keeping up with him flies away to the sweltering sky. Xavier owns this kiss. He's in control. And he's kissing me so fiercely, I have to wonder when the last time he kissed someone was. Has it been a long time? Is that why he seems so desperate. Who was the girl he kissed last? Does he miss her? Is that why he's kissing me this way?

All questions evacuate my mind, as Xavier shudders uncontrollably. I don't know why I do what I do next. Perhaps I possess some sort of kissing intuition. But whatever the reason, I find myself looping my arms around him and tracing a path down his spine in a soothing gesture. Then I slow down the kisses, moving my lips slower in an attempt to calm him down.

The attempt seems to work as Xavier's muscles unwind and his grip on me loosens. He kisses me deliberately, as if savoring every touch of our tongue, lips, and body.

Okay, this is kind of nice.

But as rapidly as the kiss started, it ends as Xavier jerks back, panting and out of air. His eyes are filled with an untamed frenzy as he carries my gaze for a desperate breath of a second. Then he takes a deep inhale and exhale and just like that, he's returned to the normal, uncaring Xavier I first met.

With a composed expression, he moves away from the car, holding onto me until I get my feet back underneath me. Then he turns toward Ralpho and Tank.

"There, are you happy?" he questions with a crook of his brow. "You got your entertainment for the day."

Ralpho gaze zeroes in on me and I don't like the way

his eyes glint. "Entertainment, huh? Who said I enjoyed that?"

"Whether you enjoyed it or not is beside the point." Benton sticks out his hand. "I think you owe us six invites and a six hour break from your perverted bullshit."

Ralpho's lip twitches in annoyance as he flicks a glance at Tank.

Tank simply shrugs then tosses a sly grin in my direction. I try not to shy away behind Benton.

Grumbling under his breath, Ralpho retrieves a small stack of red envelopes from his jacket pocket and slaps them into Benton's hand. "There's seven. Drake invited the girl too." He turns on his heels and starts toward a sleek black car parked near the front entrance of the apartment complex.

Tank gives me one final smirk before following after Ralpho. When they reach the car, Ralpho turns back at us. "You passed the test for now, but don't think this is over." He grins then climbs into the backseat of the car.

Xavier, Benton, and I remain motionless until the car peels out of the parking lot. Then Benton ushers us to get inside the car. Xavier ducks into the backseat and gives me the passenger seat. When the doors are closed, I expect an awkward silence to settle between us but instead, Benton releases a deafening breath. "

"That wasn't a fucking test." He grips the steering

wheel as he glances at Xavier in the rearview mirror. "He was fucking with us, playing a fucking mind game."

"Yeah, I know." Xavier rubs his hand across his jawline. "But I don't doubt for one minute that he wouldn't have messed up one of us if we hadn't played along."

"I know," Benton agrees, his gaze gliding to me. "It's a good thing our bad girl over here knew how to play." His lips pull to a teasing grin. "I officially take back all those sweet, cute remarks. You're kind of naughty."

My lips part in shock. "I was just doing what Jett taught me to do."

Benton's brow pops up. "Jett taught you how to do *that*?"

"What! No!" I swat his arm and he laughs. "He just taught me how to take over a situation and not lose character."

"Well, it was an interesting character you chose. Seriously, who knew you could be so bossy?" Benton's fingers fleetingly drift to his lips then he blinks a few times and starts up the engine.

"I'm sorry if I messed up," I feel the need to say as I buckle my seatbelt, guilt creeping into me. Here I'd agreed to be Benton's girlfriend and suddenly I'm kissing Xavier too. Not that I felt like I had a choice, but... I don't know. This new world I've been thrown into confuses me and honestly, I'm not sure if I'm doing the right thing or not. "I just didn't know what else to do."

"You didn't mess up," Benton assures me as he backs out of the parking space.

I breathe in relief, glad I didn't mess up. Still, that doesn't make all of my nervousness go away. Not with Xavier sitting in the back seat.

Xavier who I kissed.

Oh my gosh! Reality crashes over me. *I just kissed to guys!*

"She did good," Xavier suddenly says. For some reason, he sounds confused by this.

But hey, at least he doesn't seem pissed off at me anymore.

I don't know whether to thank him or not, if getting told I'm good at pretending to be a bad girl is a compliment, so I decide to keep my lips zipped.

The three of us grow quiet as Benton pulls out onto the road, heading toward my subdivision. Benton only speaks one time when he asks me if anyone at my house is home. When I tell him probably not, since it's Monday, he informs me that Wilder is meeting us at my house. Not wanting my family to see me show up with three guys, I send everyone a text to make sure the house is empty. Relief washes over me when I receive messages back, informing me that everyone is out and about and will be for a while.

After that, silence takes over again. I don't know

whether it's from the awkwardness of making out with them, or if they're worrying about Tank and Ralpho. And maybe even Brook, the weirdo neighbor. I want to ask questions, but I'm uncertain if I'm allowed to or not.

"Am I still supposed to be acting natural?" I whisper quietly as I crack my window to let some air in.

Benton trades another look with Xavier in the rear view mirror and Xavier retrieves his phone from his pocket. After typing a few buttons, he nods his head.

"We're good," he tells Benton, putting his phone away. "There's no bugs around, at least within a three mile radius."

"What are bugs?" I ask him.

"Recording devices that are usually secretly planted somewhere so that someone can record and eavesdrop on someone else," Xavier explains, shoving up the sleeves of his jacket.

"Oh, like in the movies?" I ask, tucking a strand of my hair behind my ear

He wavers then nods. "Pretty much."

I'll admit, I'm a bit shocked, which I guess seems sort of silly considering everything I've witnessed and learned over the past week. "I didn't realize people actually do that in real life. Well, unless you're a cop or something." I pause, my gaze skimming back and forth between Benton and Xavier. "Are you guys cops? I know you said you worked for an undercover detective program, but no one ever said if it was police related or totally separate."

Xavier catches Benton's eye and I get the impression he doesn't want Benton telling me. When Benton ignores Xavier and glances at me, Xavier crosses his arms and slumps back in the seat.

"It's not police related," Benton says. "But we do sometimes work to help the police. Like the case we're working on now. The police handed it over to the organization when they couldn't get enough proof to make the arrests."

"Proof for what?" I ask. "That these guys are drug lords?"

He nods. "That's not just it, though, which is why we haven't solved the case yet. We have enough proof that these guys are dealing and smuggling drugs, but we need to find out where the drugs are coming from, who makes them, how they're smuggling them—things like that." Keeping one hand on the steering wheel, he tensely massages the back of his neck. "There's also been speculation that Drake has been selling newly created drugs, so we need to look into that more." I must have a puzzled look on my face because he adds, "Devil's poison is a newly created drug. It has been around for a little bit, but no one knows the source of where it came from." He places both hands on the steering wheel, fixing his gaze on the road. "Our organization has shut down a few facilities that were creating new drugs and testing them out on tests subjects."

My eyes widen. "Human tests subjects?"

He nods without looking at me. "It's cruel as shit because most of the test subjects aren't there under their own free will. We've been trying to stop it, but it seems like with every facility we shut down, two more are created. And different people are running them so it's really hard to arrest everyone involved."

I shake my head, stunned. "I can't believe people would do that to other people."

"People can be very cruel sometimes," he agrees with a nod.

"Yes, they can," Xavier mumbles from the backseat, staring out the window.

I swallow hard at the pained expression on his face, wondering if someone was cruel to him. I'm not brave enough to ask him, though.

"I wish there was something I could do to help," I say, reclining back in the seat.

"You did help," Benton reassures me, giving my knee a gentle squeeze.

I give him a doubtful look. "But I haven't done anything."

"Yes, you have," he insists, leaving his hand on my knee. "You got us those invitations, which will allow us to get deeper into Drake's world."

"Which is a good thing?" Because it seems like a scary thing to me.

He bobs his head up and down, nodding. "The deeper into their world we get, the more we find out about how their system works, which will help lead us to more facilities."

"Don't you ever get scared, though? I mean, Tank and Ralpho threatened to kill one of you guys." I shudder at the thought.

He massages my knee, causing me to shudder again, but in an entirely different way that confuses me. "We won't let anything happen to you, Zhara. Me, Ridge, Jett, Jackson, Wilder, and Xavier are all going to protect you. That's a promise. And I don't make promises I can't keep."

"But who's going to protect you guys?" I ask worriedly, chewing on my thumbnail.

Benton looks from me to Xavier, his brow arching up. Xavier's eyes travel to me and he assesses me with a baffled look on his face, as if I'm an alien or something. Then he shakes his head.

"Okay, maybe you're right," he tells Benton, appearing even more befuddled.

"Right about what?" I eyeball the two of them, sensing they're talking about me.

A smile curves at Benton's lips. "That you're a sweet girl."

I start to pout, but Benton gives my leg a delicate pinch.

"No pouting, remember," he warns, but his eyes sparkle with amusement.

I blow out a dramatic sigh and cross my arms. "Fine. But that doesn't mean I like being called sweet."

"Noted." Benton's grin grows as he glances at Xavier, who appears on the verge of almost smiling.

I'm not sure I've ever seen him smile before, but when he notices me watching him, he hastily erases the amusement.

I internally sigh, wondering if there will ever be a time when he warms up to me.

"Totally off the subject, but I'm pretty sure my neighbor might be a Rogue," Benton tells Xavier as he flips on the blinker to turn into my subdivision.

Xavier slants forward, resting his elbows on his knees. "Why do you think that?"

"Because she made a discreet threat about overhearing some of us talking about certain things," Benton explains. "She didn't exactly say what those things were, but I got the impression it had to do with the organization."

"That fucking sucks. But we need to find out for sure before we make an arrest." He rubs his hand across his short, dark hair. "Is she coming to your party?"

"Well, she was until I uninvited her," Benton says, slowing the car down for a stop sign.

Xavier shakes his head. "Why the fuck did you do that? The whole point of having this party is so we could scope out your neighbors and try to figure out how many Rogues are living nearby."

So that's why he's having the party. Makes me wonder if all his other parties had ulterior motives.

"Because she was being a bitch to Zhara," Benton tells Xavier, his voice conveying a warning tone. "It was instinctive, so don't give me any shit."

"Don't give you any shit?" Xavier gapes at him. "You ruined our chance of figuring out who the Rogues are. Now we're going to have to take the time to scope her out and we don't have any extra time."

"Well, we'll make time." Benton glares at Xavier in the rear view mirror.

I don't like that they're fighting, especially since the fight was caused by me.

Swallowing hard, I straighten in my seat. "I'm sorry I caused a problem."

"You didn't cause the problem. Brook did," Benton promises me. "And Xavier knows that. He's just being an asshole."

"I'm being realistic," Xavier protests with a scowl. "We don't have any extra time to bug her place, go through her shit, and try to see if she's marked."

"Marked?" I ask. "What's that?"

Benton removes one of his hands from the steering wheel and shoves up the sleeve of his jacket, showing me a circular tattoo weaved by vines and elaborate symbols. "Every team in the organization has their own mark and every member is required to tattoo the mark on their body so that other members can identify them." He tugs down his sleeve and returns his hand to the steering wheel. "It's one way that we can identify a Rogue, by finding their mark and looking it up in the system."

"Oh." My brows dip. "Well, I'm not sure if it was a mark, but Brook did have this weird tattoo on her butt."

Benton's attention whips in my direction, his brows springing up. "When the hell did you see her ass?"

My cheeks glow with heat. "I didn't see the whole thing. Her swimsuit bottom just slid down a little when she picked up her towel." My face is so warm I'm seriously worried I might erupt in heat. "I thought you noticed."

His brow arches. "Why would I notice?"

"Because… Don't guys…" I grow flustered and start babbling. "I mean, guys check out hot girls butts all the time. At least they did with Taylor all the time. And Brook looks a lot like Taylor so I just assumed you were checking out her butt." God, I'm such a spazz.

Benton must think so too, because he chuckles. "You're seriously adorable when you do that."

Great. Now I've gone from cute to sweet to adorable.

"No, I'm not," I argue. "And a lot of people would agree with me."

"No, I think you just think a lot of people would agree with you." He extends a hand across the console and tucks a strand of my hair behind my ear. "For the record, I didn't check out Brook's ass. But I'm glad you did." He bites down on his bottom lip to keep from laughing.

I narrow my eyes at him, but I'm having a hard time not laughing. "I didn't check out her ass. She just bent over and her swimsuit started to fall down… And I…" Frustration stirs inside me as his grin widens. "It's just one of those things that you can't help looking at, like when someone is flashing a plumber's crack."

Benton smashes his lips together, fighting back a laugh. Xavier appears amused too, his eyes glittering with laughter.

I shake my head. Well, at least I got him to kind of smile.

"Whatever." I throw my hands in the air, giving up. "It doesn't really matter. I just told you because I thought maybe the tattoo could be one of those marks. And if it is, you should probably know that my neighbor has the same thing tattooed on him."

Benton's laughter dies. "Fuck."

I stiffen. "Is that bad?"

His Adam's apple bobs as he swallows hard. "I'm not sure, but yeah, it could be."

He doesn't elaborate as he pulls into the driveway of my house, leaving me to wonder just how bad it is that a Rogue is living next door to me.

DISTRACTING KISSES

Wilder is sitting on the front steps of my house when we pull up, fiddling with his phone. He's wearing a pair of black jeans, covered in zippers and the bottoms are tucked into a pair of thick, unlaced boots. The outfit is topped off with a long sleeved black shirt, a knitted cap, and leather bracelets. He looks gorgeous, but stands out and I wonder what my neighbors are thinking, if they'll tell Loki about all the guys coming into the house. Honeyton town members are known for their gossiping. But I'll just have to deal with that if the time comes because I really doubt the guys are going to let me out of their sight.

"Took you guys long enough," Wilder says as we hop out of the car. "I've been waiting here forever."

Benton rolls his eyes. "Don't be over dramatic. I know you've only been here for a few minutes."

"So?" Wilder stands to his feet and gives a glance at the sky. "It's like a hundred degrees outside. I'm practically sweating my balls off."

I don't know what sort of face I pull, but Wilder chuckles at my expression.

"I think the word 'balls' makes Zhara uncomfortable." Wilder comes up to me as I reach the stairway and drapes an arm around my shoulder. "You should probably get used to it, since Jett won't stop calling me Blue Balls." His lips tease upward. "Thanks to you."

My eyes narrow. "How was that my fault?"

"Because the only reason he started the nickname was to defend you." His eyes glimmer mischievously. "The entire situation could've been avoided if you had just let me call you Pink Cheeks."

"You wanted to call her Pink Cheeks?" Xavier asks with a bit of disgust on his face.

"Yeah, so?" Wilder shrugs. "Have you ever seen her when she gets embarrassed?"

Xavier shakes his head. "That doesn't really explain why you'd try to give her what might be the stupidest fucking nickname I've ever heard."

"You think it is, huh?" Wilder teases then turns to me. The wicked gleam in his eyes makes me try to step back from him, but he tightens his hold on my shoulder, holding me in place. "You're seriously gorgeous, Zhara." He brushes his fingers alone my cheeks. "You really are."

I think he might be trying to embarrass me so my cheeks will turn pink and Xavier will realize how fitting of a nickname Pink Cheeks is. The last thing I want is for all the guys to start calling me Pink Cheeks, so I fight the urge to get flustered, put my hands on my hips, and stare Wilder down.

"That's not going to embarrass me." But my heart argues with my words, thrashing in my chest.

He drags his piercing across his teeth again, a look of contemplation mixed with amusement rising on his expression. "Really?" He shrugs. "Guess I'm going to have to up my game then."

He dips his head and I realize he's going to kiss me. I could lean back, but for some reason I don't and his lips fuse with mine. He gives me a soft but quick kiss that sends my heart racing then he leans back. My cheeks are hotter than the damn heat wave Honeyton is having.

"What was that for?" I sputter.

Wilder chuckles, grazing his knuckles across my cheek as he glances at Xavier. "Now do you get it?"

Xavier shakes his head. "You seriously have no boundaries."

Wilder lifts a shoulder, shrugging. "Maybe you just have too many boundaries." His eyes wander to me.

"Besides, I think Zhara may have liked it." He waits for me to say something.

I open my mouth, but no words come out. I'm unsure if my silence is from not wanting to be mean and tell him I didn't like his kiss, or if deep down, I really liked. Then I mentally shake my head at myself, realizing how messed up my thoughts are.

Three guys, Zhara. You've kissed three guys within the last hour.

I swallow hard. Does that make me slutty?

I glance at Benton to see what he thinks about all of this. His eyes are trained on me, his expression indecipherable, which might be more unnerving than if he was disgusted with me.

Tearing my gaze off Benton, I step out from underneath Wilder's arm to open the front door and get everyone inside, before we give my neighbors more to gossip about. Like when Benton first came to my house, the guys start glancing at the photos of me and my family hanging on the walls. Not wanting them to see all the unflattering pictures of me, I usher them up to my room.

Halfway up the stairs, Xavier gets a phone call and heads outside to answer it, muttering that he needs to talk to the caller in private. After he leaves, we go into my bedroom, but Benton asks to use the bathroom, so Wilder and me are left alone.

Like when I was alone with Benton in my bedroom, nervousness ravels in my stomach. My nerves only escalate when Wilder stretches out on my bed and eyes over all the photos and posters on my walls, the books on my bookshelf, and my stuffed animals.

"Your room reminds me of a princess's room," he states, tucking his arms underneath his head. "Maybe that's what I'll start calling you instead of Pink Cheeks."

"You want to call me princess?" I ask, lingering near the doorway.

His lips quirk, his eyes glimmering. "What? It's not that bad."

"No, it's not," I admit. "At least compared to Pink Cheeks. But why do you have to give me a nickname at all?"

"Oh, don't pretend like you don't like it." He pats the spot beside him. "Now, stop worrying and come sit down by me for a few minutes."

My pulse quickens with fear and excitement. "I'm supposed to be changing my clothes and then Benton is taking me to the training pit."

"I know. I'm going with you." He pats the spot again. "But I promise you won't get in trouble if you lie down with me for a second." While he isn't smiling, his eyes sparkle.

He wants me to lie down beside him? On my bed!

I want to tell him no, mostly out of fear, but apparently my feet have other ideas and carry me toward the bed. I tentatively lay down beside him, keeping some space between us. But he steals the distance, scooting toward me and slipping his arm underneath my head like a makeshift pillow. Then he plays with my hair, lightly tangling his fingers through his strands.

"How are you doing with everything that happened this morning?" he asks, staring up at my ceiling.

"I'm doing okay," I say, wondering how much he knows about this morning.

He turns his head toward me, meeting my gaze. "Okay is just a placement word when people don't want to admit the truth." With his free hand, he cups my cheek. "I know what happened with Tank and Ralpho and I know that had to be fucking scary as hell for you."

"How do you know about that?" I whisper, unsure whether I feel ashamed or just confused.

One side of his mouth pulls into a half smile. "The first thing you should know about us is that we know everything."

"But how?"

"Because we're super smart," he teases with a wink.

I resist an eye roll. "No, really. How did you know about what happened? Did someone tell you?" I can't remember Benton or Xavier being on their phones much when we were in the car, but maybe they texted everyone about what happened.

He shakes his head. "Nah. We just have cameras in the parking lot and I was with Ridge, watching surveillance footage when Tank and Ralpho showed up."

My lips form an *o*, warmth rushing to my cheeks. So, not only did Tank and Ralpho watch me make out with Benton and Xavier, but Ridge and Wilder saw it.

"You don't need to be embarrassed, princess." His lip twitches at the nickname.

I shake my head, but don't protest, since I have bigger things to worry about at the moment.

"You did well in the situation," he continues while tracing his finger across my cheekbone. "And we needed you to do good because getting those invitations was important. Not to mention one of us would've been in some deep shit."

"I was really nervous," I admit. "And I'm still a little nervous about talking to Tank and Ralpho again tonight."

"That's not going to happen tonight."

"But they said I had to."

"Yeah, but that was before the distraction."

"What distraction?" I ask curiously.

"It's better if you don't know," he tells me. "But I promise you that you won't have to talk to them tonight. All you need to do for now is focus on going to the training pit and seeing your sister."

I nod, hoping he's right. That nothing else will happen. Still, my anxiety isn't completely gone. There are so many unanswered questions about my family. Not to mention, my neighbor might be a Rogue. Plus, Drake invited me to his masquerade ball, which means that in the future I'm going to have to meet another drug lord.

Sensing my worry, he strokes my cheek with his fingers. "Everything will be fine, princess. I promise."

I nod, but doubt weighs on my shoulders.

Wilder sighs. "You know what, I think you need a distraction." He mulls over something then a wicked smile curls at his lips. "And I think I have the perfect idea." He leans in, as if to kiss me.

I freeze, my heart pounding in my chest. "What're you doing?"

"Kissing you." Hilarity rings in his tone. "Wasn't that obvious?"

"Yeah, but what isn't obvious is why?"

"I already said—to distract you, which FYI, kissing and tongue rings can be very distracting." A playful smile tugs at his lips. "I thought it was pretty obvious what I was doing, but apparently I need to work on my game." He winks at me. "Don't tell Jackson I said that, though."

I can't help but smile. But the smile fades as he leans in to kiss me. I could move away. In fact, I probably should. But instead, I lie there, watching his lips near mine. I don't know what kind of girl that makes me. A bad one? A confused one? The answer is unclear and the question disappears as his lips near mine.

But then suddenly he's slanting back.

"Fuck." He jumps off the bed and rushes toward the window.

Dazed and confused, I sit up, worried I did something wrong. But then I see a red light shining through the window and realize something is *really* wrong.

Because I've seen that light before, coming from the next-door neighbors.

Aka, Creepy Charles place.

Ducking to the floor, Wilder lets out another string of curses as he digs his phone out of his pocket. "Zhara, stay low and lie down on the floor," he orders as he punches buttons on his phone.

I do as he says, rolling off the bed and lying on the floor on my stomach. "What is that light?"

"A scanner." He doesn't embellish. "Shit, Benton's not answering."

I start to ask him what a scanner is when he army crawls toward the door, nodding for me to follow. "Keep low and follow me."

I drag my body across the floor, following him out of my room.

Once we're in the hallway, he leaps up, snags my arm, and lifts me to my feet. Then he tows me with him as he hauls butt down the hallway toward the stairway. Fear pulsates through my body, questions racing through my mind over what a scanner could be and why Wilder seems so afraid of it.

But as we reach the middle of the stairs, my attention is pulled to Benton.

He's standing in the foyer, holding his phone up next to a photo of me of when I was younger. He must have his phone on speakerphone, since he's talking in a hushed whisper to someone. Well, either that or he's talking to himself. Wilder doesn't seem to notice any of this, his attention fixed on the screen of his phone, which has lit up with a glowing red light.

Strange. Almost as strange as what Benton is doing.

A sense of dread settles in my stomach. I don't know why, but I have a terrible feeling something bad is about to happen.

As we near the bottom of the stairs, I get a better glimpse of Benton's phone and stop dead in my tracks, the sense of dread amplifying.

"Why do you have a photo of me when I was younger on your phone?" I ask, gripping onto the banister.

Benton whirls around, startled, while Wilder's head whips up.

"Shit," Wilder says at the same time Benton hurries to put his phone away.

"What was that?" I ask worriedly. Because it looked like a photo of me attached to some sort of file.

Benton trades a nervous look with Wilder before his gaze settles on me. "It's something you don't need to worry about right now."

I've never been one to demand the truth, but that sense of dread consumes me.

Something isn't right. What if it has to do with my parents? Has he found out something—something bad—and isn't telling me.

Wiggling my hand from Wilder's, I take a step toward Benton. "No, I want to worry about it right now."

Benton carries my gaze, swallowing hard. Then his lips part. "We've been keeping some stuff from you—"

"He can't tell you right now," Wilder cuts him off. "Not with an SC."

Benton's eyes briefly widen. "*What?*"

Wilder points up at the ceiling. "Right now."

They're speaking in code and it's driving me crazy, mainly because Benton just admitted that he's been keeping some stuff from me. But I have a feeling they're not talking normally because a scanner might be similar to being bugged.

"We should go," Wilder says. "Take a bit of a break then regroup. You can take her to the T. It should be good there."

Benton nods once then reaches for my hand, but I step back. He freezes, giving me a worried look.

"Zhara, please." His eyes beg for me to cooperate.

I don't want to and if I were in bad girl character, I wouldn't. But, without the guys, I'd be alone in this. And that scares me.

So, I take his hand and allow him to lead me outside to his car. Wilder and Xavier climb into the backseat while I take the passenger seat. No one speaks as we back out onto the road, but I send a text to Alexis, wishing she'd answer—wishing I had someone else to talk to about this. But I get no response and an uneasiness stews inside me. The last update I got about her was from Benton and apparently he hasn't been honest with me. What if Alexis isn't okay? What if no one in my family is safe? And why the heck did Benton have that photo of me on his phone?

After we drive out of the neighborhood, I turn to Benton to ask him questions. But he shakes his head and points at my arm.

I glance down to see what he's pointing at and then my jaw nearly smacks my knees. Underneath my pale, freckled skin, my blood veins have become extremely defined and dark.

"What's happening to me?" I whisper in horror, tears stinging my eyes.

Benton's jaw sets tight as he looks back at the road. "I'll explain later, but I promise you'll be okay."

Wilder said okay was a placement word, so what is Benton not telling me. Apparently a lot of stuff.

Just how many lies have I been told?

My stomach churns at the possible answers and all I want to do is get out of the car and run. But, not having any place to run to, I have no choice but to stay in the car and hope that whatever secrets Benton has been keeping from me aren't as bad as I think.

But as the veins on my arms continue to darken and my body turns cold, I know my own thoughts are lying to me. That this is probably going to be as bad as I think.

Maybe even worse.

BENTON

This is probably the worse way Zhara could've found out that she was once a test patient in a Drug Tunnel Experimental Facility, which is what the photo I had confirmed. I was planning on telling her later, after we got back to my house where we'd be able to talk privately. But now I'm going to have to explain everything to her when we get to the training pit, which isn't the ideal place to tell a girl that she was once used for testing new drugs. She's going to have a lot of questions, like why she ended up in the facility and under an alias name. And why on earth her blood veins are darkening right now. The first two questions I can't answer yet, although I fully plan on looking into them. The latter I do have an answer for unfortunately. Her body is reacting to the scan that I'm assuming her neighbor did. A scan can detect just about everything, giving x-ray vision along with reflecting sounds, which means anyone doing a scan can see and hear whatever they want. Scanners are very rare and it makes me wonder what sort of connection her neighbor has.

Scanners have side effects too, one being it counteracts with certain types of electronic chips. Which means, Zhara has an electronic chip planted in her. It could be from her time at the facility. But I was under the impression the organization removed the chips after they rescued the subjects. So now I'm wondering if someone else planted a chip on her.

Telling her this isn't going to be easy, especially since I promised her everything will be okay.

I need to fix this. Somehow.

I just hope she gives me the time to fix it.

Out of the corner of my eye, I glance at her, trying to get a vibe on what she's thinking.

She's staring at her arms, her face pale, her eyes crammed with hurt. I hate that I'm part of the reason the hurt is there. Hate that I hurt her. Hate that the morning turned out this way. She'd done so well with Tank and Ralpho situation , even if watching her kiss Xavier did make my jaw tick a bit. He won't admit it, but he enjoyed the kiss, even if it was all supposed to be a show. Xavier rarely shows emotion—well, other than being pissed off at the world—but his guard went down during the kiss. It's been a long time since his guard has gone down.

"This will go away, right?" Zhara suddenly whispers, tracing her fingertip across her blood veins.

I nod my head once, worried we're still too close to the scanner. "You're going to be fine, sweetheart."

She doesn't look relieved, her skin paling even more.

Not knowing how else to comfort her, I reach across the console and lace my fingers through her's. I expect her to pull away and wouldn't blame her if she did, but she surprises me when she leaves her hand in mine.

The gesture gives me a drop of hope that when I tell her the truth she won't fucking run for the hills. She can't run, even if she wants to. Sadly she's in our world too deeply to run away now and part of me hates myself for bringing her into this mess. But at the same time, I think the mess would've eventually found her anyway.

I just wish I knew who brought Zhara into a world full of drug lords, organizations, and why the hell she ended up in the Drug Tunnel Experimental Facility to begin with.

ABOUT THE AUTHOR

Jessica Sorensen is a *New York Times* and *USA Today* best-selling author who lives in the snowy mountains of Wyoming. When she's not writing, she spends her time reading and hanging out with her family.

Cursed Hadley

Enchanting Hadley (coming soon)

<u>Tangled Realms:</u>

Forever Violet

Untitled (coming soon)

<u>Curse of the Vampire Queen:</u>

Tempting Raven

Enchanting Raven

Alluring Raven

Untitled (coming soon)

<u>Unraveling You Series:</u>

Unraveling You

Raveling You

Awakening You

Inspiring You

Fated by Darkness

Untitled (coming soon)

<u>Unexpected Series:</u>

The Unexpected Way of Falling

The Unpredictable Way of Falling

Untitled (coming soon)

<u>Shadow Cove Series:</u>

What Lies in the Darkness

What Lies in the Dark

Untitled (coming soon)

<u>Mystic Willow Bay Series:</u>

The Secret Life of a Witch

Broken Magic

Untitled (coming soon)

<u>Standalones:</u>

The Forgotten Girl

The Illusion of Annabella

Confessions of a Kleptomaniac

Rules of a Rebel and a Shy Girl

The Opposite of Ordinary

<u>Broken City Series:</u>

Nameless

Forsaken

Oblivion

Forbidden (coming soon)

<u>Guardian Academy Series:</u>

Entranced

Entangled

Enchanted

Entice (coming soon)

<u>Sunnyvale Series:</u>

The Year I Became Isabella Anders

The Year of Falling in Love

The Year of Second Chances

<u>The Coincidence Series:</u>

The Coincidence of Callie and Kayden

The Redemption of Callie and Kayden

The Destiny of Violet and Luke

The Probability of Violet and Luke

The Certainty of Violet and Luke

The Resolution of Callie and Kayden

Seth & Greyson

<u>The Secret Series:</u>

The Prelude of Ella and Micha

The Secret of Ella and Micha

The Forever of Ella and Micha

The Temptation of Lila and Ethan

The Ever After of Ella and Micha

Lila and Ethan: Forever and Always

Ella and Micha: Infinitely and Always

The Shattered Promises Series:

Shattered Promises

Fractured Souls

Unbroken

Broken Visions

Scattered Ashes

Breaking Nova Series:

Breaking Nova

Saving Quinton

Delilah: The Making of Red

Nova and Quinton: No Regrets

Tristan: Finding Hope

Wreck Me

Ruin Me

The Fallen Star Series:

The Fallen Star

The Underworld

The Vision

The Promise

The Lost Soul

The Evanescence

The Darkness Falls Series:

Darkness Falls

Darkness Breaks

Darkness Fades

The Death Collectors Series (NA and YA):

Ember X and Ember

Cinder X and Cinder

Spark X and Spark

Unbeautiful Series:

Unbeautiful

Untamed

www.ingramcontent.com/pod-product-compliance
Lightning Source LLC
Chambersburg PA
CBHW032030180726
48284CB00008B/2545